"W

Josi... he got his... that when he was ten his collie died, and he ...ed the gravestone himself."

The lawyer's eyes widened slightly. "Anyone could know those things."

"No," a harsh voice came from the doorway. "Not anyone."

The lawyer leaned forward. "Chase!"

Josie felt nauseated again. Who was this? Were they trying to fool her, bringing in someone to pose as Chase and hope she'd snap at the bait?

"It was Chase who told me."

"That's a lie. Until you wrecked your car in my driveway, I had never seen you before in my life."

He sounded…so certain. So indignant. So exactly how an honest man unjustly accused would sound. Suddenly she understood. The dashing heartbreaker she'd met and the tenderhearted rancher's son whose stories had won her heart…they were two different men.

"Damn it. Say something."

She met his furious gaze helplessly. She had nothing to say. Not to him. All she could possibly say was…

"I'm so sorry, Mr Clayton. I've never seen you, either."

Dear Reader,

Having a baby is one of the most exciting things a woman can do – and one of the most terrifying. A new human being is taking shape inside you, a child who will own your heart and change your life. Yet you have no idea what this new person will be like. Sometimes we're mature enough to think about the genetic implications of the man we pick to father our children. More often, I'd suspect, we're just swept away, by love or lust, or the hope of relief from loneliness.

Josie Whitford was hungry for all those things. And now, too late, she discovers that she doesn't know who the father of her child really is. But then she meets Chase Clayton, the handsome rancher who is everything her lover wasn't. As they search for the man who abandoned her, she begins to have second thoughts about what makes a "father." Is it possible that birth is only the beginning?

Yes, a father can give you curly hair and brown eyes. But he can also give you love and patience, wisdom and courage and, above all, time. Time spent telling bedtime stories, explaining photosynthesis, kissing away tears. His constancy can make you confident. His strength can make you brave. His compassion can make you kind. Chase Clayton could be that kind of father. But Josie's already pregnant, and he's engaged to someone else. Surely it's too late for them.

Or is it? Is it possible that love really can conquer all?

I hope you enjoy their story.

Warmly,

Kathleen

Texas Baby

KATHLEEN O'BRIEN

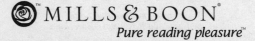

MILLS & BOON®
Pure reading pleasure™

All the characters in this book have no existence outside the
imagination of the author, and have no relation whatsoever to anyone
bearing the same name or names. They are not even distantly inspired
by any individual known or unknown to the author, and all the
incidents are pure invention.

First published in Great Britain 2009
by Harlequin Mills & Boon Limited,
Eton House, 18-24 Paradise Road, Richmond, Surrey TW9 1SR

ISBN: 978 0 263 87354 2

38-0109

Harlequin Mills & Boon policy is to use papers that are
natural, renewable and recyclable products and made from
wood grown in sustainable forests. The logging and
manufacturing processes conform to the legal environmental
regulations of the country of origin.

Printed and bound in Spain
by Litografia Rosés S.A., Barcelona

ABOUT THE AUTHOR

If you could own any horse, it would be... (um, would someone else muck out the stalls?) If so, then Tornado, Zorro's beautiful black Andalusian. **John Wayne or Gary Cooper?** Cooper, of course! "Don't shove me, Harv. I'm tired of being shoved." **Favourite Western?** *Butch Cassidy and the Sundance Kid.* **Best name for a horse?** Merrylegs, from *Black Beauty.* **Cowboys are your weakness because...** I love a man who can do, will do and doesn't ever complain. **What makes the cowboy?** It's the hat. Think James Dean in *Giant.* Oh, what a perfect tilt can do to a woman!

CHAPTER ONE

IT WAS ONE OF THOSE MORNINGS.

No, Josie Whitford corrected herself as she poured another round of coffee into Mr. Benetta's cup, smiling even though she had a hammering headache, that was a laughable understatement.

It was one of those *years*. The ones in which you just couldn't catch a break, couldn't get ahead, couldn't even run fast enough to stay in place. Ones where you felt yourself stumbling, slipping backward, as if life were a treadmill set on the highest speed, programmed to cycle out the weak.

Of course, the morning itself was lousy, too. Raindrops as fat as marbles, true Texas raindrops, bounced off the oily pavement, and the windows of the Not Guilty Café had turned gray and runny. They reminded Josie of the last plate she'd carried to the kitchen, prune juice splashed into the remnants of over-easy eggs. For a minute, just remembering, she thought she might get sick.

Oh, God, she wasn't finally catching that flu, was she? She'd managed to avoid it all winter, but lately she'd been so run-down, so damn tired. The splat of gravy on her apron, courtesy of the kid at table two, sent up a wave of odor, and the banana she'd had for breakfast rose in her throat.

No. She clamped her jaw. *Not on the customer.* That would be the perfect excuse to fire her, the one Ed had been waiting for.

She pivoted away from Mr. Benetta, breathing through her mouth to avoid the smell of bacon grease wafting from the grill. The Not Guilty Café didn't use the best cuts of anything, but it had the benefit of a great location. Tucked into the shadow of Riverfork City Hall and courthouse for the past fifty years, the café had become a tradition for the local politicians, businessmen and lawyers.

For a minute, she just stood there, the coffeepot hot against her hand, the banana roiling in her stomach. She looked around, panicked, but oddly paralyzed. On a day like this, when the rain made a good excuse for arriving late to work, the customers lingered, and the café was jammed. Where could she throw up without having to pay someone's dry cleaning bill?

Nowhere. She felt sweat break out on her forehead even as a chill passed across her back, from shoulder to shoulder. She set down the coffeepot, which suddenly felt as heavy as an anchor.

Oh, how she wanted to go home. She longed for a nap, for the soothing warmth of the expensive sheets Chase had bought her that day in the Galleria. Sometimes, when she snuggled down into the five-hundred-thread cocoon, she could imagine that Chase, with his hot hands and his hard body, was still lying there beside her.

That she wasn't completely alone.

But she *was* alone. And unless she intended to sell those sheets to pay next semester's tuition, she'd better stay put, chills or no chills. She needed every penny she could make today. And then some.

"Hey, gal, come out of that trance. Is your blood sugar low? Table six is getting cranky. And you know Ed's watching."

Josie snapped to attention, anxiety taking precedence over nausea. She tossed Marlene, her favorite coworker, a grateful grimace, then glanced toward the front register, where Ed stood, giving her the evil eye.

The bastard. If she was exhausted, it was his fault. He'd been working her double shifts for weeks, seating all the most demanding customers in her section, riding her like a devil. No one could keep that pace, and he knew it. He would torment her as long as he could, for the sheer fun of it, and then he'd fire her.

"Don't let him get to you, hon." Marlene leaned in, her shoulder warm against Josie's, her voice a raspy whisper. "You know he's just cranky 'cause he can't get into your pants."

Josie nodded, though that wasn't exactly true. Ed was angry, all right. But he wasn't upset just because Josie always told him *no*. What made him positively rabid was that she'd told Chase Clayton *yes*.

Fat lot of good that had done her. At least if she'd slept with Ed she might have gotten a raise and some decent shifts. Sleeping with Chase Clayton hadn't left her with anything but a bruised heart, a cynical attitude toward romantic dreams and a C on her English lit exam—her first C in four long years at the community college.

And, of course, a set of supersoft sheets.

Maybe her blood sugar *was* low. She felt tearful suddenly, just at the thought of Chase, which was really dumb. He'd been gone for two months now, twice as long as the fairy tale had lasted in the first place.

She dug in her pocket for a glucose tablet and popped it surreptitiously into her mouth. Ed saw, of course, though he probably thought it was gum, or an aspirin. Marlene was the only one who knew about her diabetes and the shots she'd taken every day since she was a kid.

Frowning, Ed called her name out in a booming voice. He always talked like a radio announcer, probably to compensate for being shaped like a stick of spaghetti. And maybe other shortcomings, as well. There must be a reason the waitresses secretly called him "pinkie."

"Josie!" He made a circular "hurry up" motion with his hand. He pointed toward the waiting area, a ten-square-foot nook where some of the biggest deals in River-fork politics were forged by big, red-faced men with soft drawls, Stetson hats and lizard-skin boots.

It wasn't Josie's turn to straighten the area, and, just as Marlene warned her, the dad at table six was tapping his menu and shooting her dirty looks, but she knew better than to argue with Ed.

Still, there might be trouble, and she didn't have the energy to cope with it today. The dad looked like an Alpha male and would undoubtedly complain about her slow service. Ed obviously expected that—wanted it, even. He had a stack of write-ups on her now, and when he got tired of torturing her, he'd stuff them down her throat.

She should quit.

But even that took more energy than she had today.

As she gathered old, crumpled paper coffee cups, dirty stir sticks and torn straw wrappers, she felt Ed's gaze crawl across her back like bugs.

She took shallow breaths, trying not to smell the old, spilled coffee. Though her hands shook, she moved aside the mints and the rumpled newspaper sections, which felt clammy, absorbing the stormy air. Putting those back together would take forever, but she might as well get started.

Ed was a fool to keep the customers waiting, just to play this power trip on her. Someday one of them would complain to the owners, and he'd learn that managers could lose their jobs, too.

That ought to please her, but somehow

it didn't. She couldn't really feel anything but this pulsing nausea. She ought to start stumping for a new job. She ought to sue him for sexual harassment.

But the very idea of any of those things felt like climbing a jagged, frozen mountain. She couldn't even summon up enough indignation to hate him right now.

What on earth was wrong with her? She wondered if her insulin dose might be out of whack after all. Surely this weary exhaustion wasn't completely emotional. Surely it wasn't all about Chase Clayton.

Coming home to find her fairy-tale lover vanished, her idyll smashed, had been painful, but not completely crushing. As beautiful as the fantasy had been, she'd always known it couldn't last. A rich, handsome rancher with 25,000 acres romancing a twenty-five-year-old waitress struggling to make her rent and finish community college?

Yeah, right. Everyone knew how *that* story ended.

So, though it had hurt, she'd fully

expected to nurse her bruised heart and childish disappointment for a while, then dust herself off and get back to work.

But instead of feeling a little stronger every week, she'd actually been sinking, going deeper each day into this shadowy hole of lethargy. Last night she'd been so depressed she had even picked up the phone and begun calling her mother's house in Austin.

Luckily, she'd come to her senses before the last number was punched. Her hands had trembled as she put down the receiver, grateful for the near miss. Suppose her stepfather had answered? He'd warned her she couldn't make it on her own. She'd spent the past seven years proving him wrong, by God, and she wasn't going to give up now.

She picked up the sports section, the most pawed-over of the lot, naturally, and rearranged the pages. Then she added the front page, with its war news and bold black headlines predicting bird flu, rising murder rates and new taxes.

She closed her eyes, fighting back another wave of nausea.

It must be the flu. Maybe she'd better see the doctor next time Ed gave her a day off. If he ever did.

Finally she located the feature section, which had been folded inside out. The page on top was all weddings and engagements, row upon row of finger-sized pictures of beautiful young women who radiated confidence and optimism, as if they were lit by the shimmer of their engagement diamonds. As if they'd been sprinkled with the magic dust of True Love.

She squeezed the paper so hard it bent and softened in her damp fist. How lovely it would be to feel like that. Adored, pampered, beaming. Your whole life in front of you, and a loving partner to stand beside you, in sickness and in health.

To know that you would never be alone again.

"I've transferred table six to Marlene," Ed said, his swollen voice suddenly right behind her shoulder. "They were ready to get up and leave. For God's sake, I had no idea cleaning up over here would take you so long."

Yes, you did, she wanted to cry out. But vomit closed off her throat, and a deep heaviness flowed into her veins, as if she'd been injected with mud. She didn't even look at him. She kept her eyes on the happy women, the healthy, happy women standing on the threshold of paradise.

Aleshia Phillips to marry Timothy Braxton.

Sandra Culter to marry Arthur Brun.

Susannah Everly to marry Chase Clayton.

What?

Her heart stopped. She tried to take in air, but her throat wasn't working, either.

Susannah Everly to marry Chase Clayton.

No.

Chase Clayton.

Josie felt her head bobbing, as if her heart beat so hard it shook her whole body with every stroke. She saw her own brown bangs, which needed cutting. They looked dull and lank as they trembled across her vision. She tried to think, but none of the gears in her brain seemed willing to turn.

She held out one hand toward Ed. "I," she began, strangling the word. "I—"

He had no pity, as usual. He looked annoyed by her incoherence. He shifted, and his cologne filled the air. "Jeez, Josie, get a grip."

And then, finally, she lost the battle, all the battles. With her pride, with her heart, her exhaustion, and even, to Ed's dismay, her roiling stomach.

"I—" She tried one more time.

And then she threw up all over his lizard-skin boots.

CHAPTER TWO

TWO HOURS into his own engagement party, Chase Clayton was bored and restless and having trouble hiding it.

He had agreed to put on a tie and make nice with all their friends for Susannah's sake—she loved parties—but the truth was, he was bored stiff.

Besides, there was work he needed to do. Well, *needed* might be an exaggeration. Trent, his ranch manager, was too good to leave much for Chase to worry about.

But there was work he'd *rather* do. Every time another person in this endless line of well-wishers came up, slapped him on the back and offered the same carbon copy congratulations, he smiled politely, but his mind was a mile away, wondering how things were going on the reroofing of the south stable.

When his phone vibrated on his belt, it was like getting a governor's reprieve. He eased back his jacket and sneaked a peek at the text. Trent had a problem and needed a minute. Chase could say no, but he wasn't going to. Fate had thrown him a life raft, and he was jumping on.

"Would you excuse me? That call was from Trent. Some kind of hay emergency, if you can believe there is such a thing." Chase smiled at Jenny Wilcox, the pastor's wife, who for some unknown reason seemed to be so damn happy about Chase's engagement that she'd spent the past twenty minutes alternately giggling and then tearing up like a leaky faucet.

"Of course. I've kept you from Susannah far too long," Jenny said, sniffing in a bliss of emotion. "Oh, I'm so pleased that you two finally got together! You're so perfect together. And with the ranches right next door…oh, it's just too perfect!"

Before another spill of tears could

appear, Chase squeezed her hand and turned away. Trying not to attract attention, he set down his tumbler of ice water and eased toward the corner of the terrace. He wondered, just for a second, whether Trent had manufactured this crisis. He knew Chase well, and might have guessed that his boss needed a breather.

Or maybe it had something to do with Sue. Chase looked over his shoulder. Susannah Everly stood by the fountain talking to Jim Stilling, their lawyer. She held a glass of white wine that caught the sunshine when she drank, tossing it in gold sparkles onto her strong, tanned shoulders. Jim seemed mesmerized, and even Chase had to admit that Sue looked great. That low-cut green dress was the girliest outfit he'd ever seen her wear, and he'd known her all her life.

Any man in his right mind would be thrilled to marry a woman like that.

The man he was about to meet, for instance. Trent Maxwell had loved Susannah for years.

Which showed how Fate enjoyed a little kick of irony, didn't it?

Chase slipped around the edge of the terrace. As the chatter of voices faded, he strolled to the front of the house, ignoring the small twinge of conscience at being absent from his own celebration.

All through his childhood, he'd been infamous for sneaking away from family parties. His parents had thrown the biggest balls and barbecues in the county. Anything was an excuse for a Clayton festival— Christmas, birthdays, Chase's elementary school graduation, the full moon...*anything*. But Chase always found himself bored, drifting down to the riverbank to catch minnows, or into the stables to brush Captain Kirk, the lazy bald-face bay his parents had given him when he'd turned fourteen.

"You sure you're a Clayton, son?" His father, a huge, happy man, loved to snag his young son by the feet. "You sure your mom didn't slip the corral about nine months before you were born?" He'd check

Chase's heel, just for the pride of seeing the walnut-colored Clayton birthmark. "Yep, you've got the family brand, but I'll be damned if I know where this antisocial stuff sneaked into the bloodline."

It had sneaked in, though. Chase and Trent had been friends since elementary school, and Chase sometimes wondered whether they had been accidentally switched at birth. Trent was suave and well dressed, socially sought after, the ideal guest. Chase preferred blue jeans and hard work, and the company of horses.

"Hey, corporal, over here," a voice said, and Chase looked toward the front porch. Trent stood in the shadows, leaning over the balcony, his shoulders oddly stiff. He hadn't turned his head in Chase's direction. Instead, he seemed half-frozen, staring out toward the road.

Chase wondered what Trent was looking at. The main house fronted pretty close to the street, so this view wasn't the one that took your breath away.

The real beauty was from the back,

where the party was going on right now. The Double C was substantial, but not grand—25,000 acres now that Chase had bought the Hillman land—and, behind the house, acre after acre of green pasture and ponderosa pines undulated down to the creek. Clayton land splashed right through the clear, pebbled water and then marched across another ten thousand acres of peach orchard, almost all the way to the Austin city limits.

Out here, though, there wasn't much to see, unless you counted the bluebonnets on either side of the white fence that marked the half-mile driveway. But as Chase drew closer, he got a better view of Trent's face. He realized his friend hadn't been looking at anything. He'd just been staring blind.

Of course. This wasn't going to be an easy day for Trent, no matter how you cut it.

Chase climbed the six steps and joined his manager on the porch, leaning his elbows on the banister, too. "So, what's up? Is there really a hay emergency, or are you playing guardian angel, giving me a breather?"

Trent laughed. "Both. About the hay—
we went with that new company you said
you wanted. Old Joe's daughter's new
business. She delivered a semi load today,
and the first three bales were moldy."

Trent's educated voice was clipped,
clearly irritated. He didn't tolerate moldy
hay, or any other kind of shabby work,
which was what made him the perfect ranch
manager. He was what cowboys used to
call "square." Completely on top of his job.

"Damn it." Chase whistled through his
teeth and scuffed a toe against the balus-
trade. "I really wanted to throw her some
business. Joe asked me to, and you know
he wouldn't ask a river for water if he were
dying of thirst."

"That's why I called. Ordinarily, I'd just
send it back and get another hay company.
We don't give second chances. But since
she's old Joe's daughter…"

"Yeah." *Hell's bells.* Chase knew he was
without options here. Joe had been ranch
manager for two generations of Claytons,
and he'd reluctantly retired when Chase's

dad had died five years ago. But the old guy had dropped enough of his sweat on Clayton soil that Chase would always feel beholden. "Okay. Just this one time. She gets a do-over."

Trent glanced at him, his mouth a one-cornered smile. "Somehow that's what I thought you'd say."

Chase smiled, too. Trent wasn't kidding anybody. This little decision definitely hadn't required a face-to-face. He'd just been saving Chase's ass, and Chase appreciated it. Their business was done, but he didn't move. He didn't want to go back.

For a couple of minutes, they stood together in silence, watching the leaves of the sweet gum tree carve shapes on the front yard. In some intangible way, the silence wasn't as companionable as it used to be, before Chase's engagement.

He wondered if Trent was ready to talk about it. For the past month, they'd both pretty much pretended it wasn't happening.

Finally, without taking his gaze from the

grass, Trent spoke. "So. How's it going back there? I saw her. She looks happy."

Chase made a noncommittal sound. This was tricky territory they were stepping over, and he wasn't sure of his footing. "I guess she is. That ranch means a lot to her. If it meant she could keep it, she probably would have married the devil himself."

Shit. Two seconds into this conversation, and Chase already had a mouthful of foot. "Hell, Trent. You know what I mean."

"Yeah. She would have married anyone." Trent straightened up and met Chase's gaze. He shrugged in that elegant way that drove most women mad. "Anyone but me."

It was so true, there was no way to contradict it. So Chase didn't try. Every word he thought of had a "quicksand" warning sign posted all over it. Better, when you didn't have the gift of gab, to shut the hell up.

He considered laying his hand on Trent's shoulder, but that seemed patronizing, too.

Apparently Trent agreed. He took a deep breath, then began descending the porch stairs. He paused at the bottom. "You heading back now? You probably should, you know. If your mom was here, she would've had a fit if she saw you leave your own party."

Trent was right there, too. Chase's mother had come from Virginia, and she'd had very strict ideas about how her son should behave. She didn't mind his quiet nature, but whenever he was rude she'd always "explained" his mistake to him so gently and sweetly he ended up wanting to shoot himself.

"In a minute," Chase said. "I need a little time alone. Jenny Wilcox was talking my ear off."

Finally Trent smiled. "Your mom always said trying to teach a Texan manners was like trying to teach a snake to tap-dance."

"Yeah. But she never had to talk to Jenny Wilcox."

Trent chuckled, but still hesitated.

"Look, Trent," Chase said, feeling oddly defensive. "I don't plan to saddle up and ride off into the sunset. I'm not going to back out on her. I just want a few minutes alone."

"Okay," Trent said. "Just don't…" He frowned. "Don't stay out here so long it ends up embarrassing her."

Chase nodded. "Never," he said solemnly. He held Trent's gaze. "That's a promise."

After Trent was gone, the minutes stretched out quietly, interrupted only by the carrying-on of the robins and the wind flirting with the sweet gum tree. Chase let his tired gaze rest on the bluebonnets, which were blooming their hearts out today.

They should have held the party out here. Susannah had the terrace decorated like something out of a magazine, lots of cute ribbons and potted plants shaped like illustrations from geometry textbooks. But for his money you couldn't beat the first big honest splash of spring flowers.

He felt his chest relaxing. His breath came deeper, from the gut, where it was supposed to. After a few more minutes, he was a little sun-stunned, and when he heard a strange noise in the distance he wasn't completely sure he wasn't dreaming.

But then he transferred his gaze to the road and identified a foreign spot on the horizon. A car. Almost half a mile away, where the straight, tree-lined drive met the public road. He could tell it was coming too fast, but judging the speed of a vehicle moving straight toward you was tricky.

It wasn't until it was about two hundred yards away that he realized the driver must be drunk…or crazy. Or both.

The guy was going maybe sixty. On a private drive, where kids or horses or tractors or stupid chickens might come darting out any minute, that was criminal. Chase straightened from his comfortable slouch and waved his hands.

"Slow down, you fool," he called. He took the porch steps quickly and began walking fast down the driveway.

The car veered, from one side to the other, then up onto the slight rise of the thick green spring grass. It barely missed the fence.

"Slow down, damn it!"

He couldn't see the driver, but he definitely didn't recognize the automobile. It was small and old and hadn't cost much even when it was new. It used to be white, but now it needed either a wash or a new paint job or both.

"Goddamn it, what's wrong with you?"

At the last minute, he had to jump away, because the idiot behind the wheel clearly wasn't going to turn to avoid a collision. He couldn't believe it. The car kept coming, finally slowing a little, but it was too late.

Still going about thirty miles an hour, it slammed into the large, white-brick pillar that marked the front boundaries of the house. The pillar wasn't going to give an inch, so that car had to. The front end folded up like a paper fan.

It seemed to take forever for the car to settle, as if the trauma happened in slow motion, reverberating from the front to the back of the car in ripples of destruction. The front windshield seemed to ice over with lethal bits of glassy frost. Then the side windows exploded.

The front driver's door wrenched open, as if the car wanted to expel its contents.

Metal buckled hideously. Small pieces like hubcaps skipped and ricocheted insanely across the oyster-shell driveway.

Finally, everything was still. Into the silence, a plume of steam shot up like a geyser, smelling of rust and heat. Its snake-like hiss almost smothered the low, agonized moan of the driver.

Chase's anger had disappeared. He didn't feel anything but a dull sense of dis-belief. Things like this didn't happen in real life. Not in his life. Maybe the sun had actually put him to sleep.

But he was already kneeling beside the car. The driver was a woman. There was no air bag. The frosty glass of the wind-shield was dotted with small flecks of blood. She must have hit it with her head, because just below her hairline a red liquid was seeping out. He touched it. He tried to wipe it away before it reached her eyebrow, though of course that made no sense at all. Her eyes were shut.

Was she conscious? Did he dare move her? Her dress was covered in glass, and the metal of the car was sticking out dangerously in all the wrong places.

Then he remembered, with an intense relief, that every good medical man in the county was here, just behind the house, drinking his champagne. He found his phone and paged Trent.

The woman moaned again.

Alive, then. Thank God for that.

He saw Trent coming toward him, starting out at a lope, but switching to a full run when he saw the car.

"Get Dr. Marchant," Chase called. "Don't bother with 911."

Trent didn't take long to assess the situation. A fraction of a second, and he began pulling out his cell phone and running toward the house.

The yelling seemed to have roused the woman. She opened her eyes. They were blue, and clouded with pain and confusion.

"Chase," she said.

His breath stalled. His head pulled back. "What?"

Her only answer was another moan, and

he wondered if he had imagined the word. He reached around her and put his arm behind her shoulders. She was tiny. Probably petite by nature, but surely way too thin. He could feel her shoulder blades pushing against her skin, as fragile as the wishbone in a turkey.

She seemed to have passed out, so he put his other arm under her knees and lifted her from the car. He tried to avoid the jagged metal, but her skirt caught on a piece and the tearing sound seemed to wake her again.

"No," she said. "Please."

"I'm just trying to help," he said. "It's going to be all right."

She seemed profoundly distressed. She wriggled in his arms, and she was so weak, like a broken bird. It made him feel too big and brutish. And intrusive. As if touching her this way, his bare hands against the warm skin behind her knees, were somehow a transgression.

He wished he could be more delicate.

But he smelled gasoline, and he knew it wasn't safe to leave her.

Finally he heard the sound of voices, as guests began to run around the side of the house, alerted by Trent. Dr. Marchant was at the front, racing toward them as if he were forty instead of seventy. Susannah was right behind him, her green dress floating around her trim legs.

"Please," the woman in his arms murmured again. She looked at him, the expression in her blue eyes lost and bewildered. He wondered if she might be on drugs. Hitting her head on the windshield might account for this unfocused, glazed look, but it couldn't explain the crazy driving.

"Please, put me down. Susannah… This wedding…"

Chase's arms tightened instinctively, and he froze in his tracks. She whimpered, and he realized he might be hurting her. "Say that again?"

"The wedding. I have to stop it."

CHAPTER THREE

CHASE ENDURED the next hour the way he'd endured most of the crises in his life—he kept busy.

He played host the best he could. He soothed the hysterical—Jenny Wilcox was hyperventilating and her husband, Pastor Wilcox, wasn't far behind. He deflected the curious. He tried to get as many guests as possible to go home. This became much more difficult once the rumor began to circulate that the mysterious woman lying upstairs in the north guest room, being tended by Dr. Marchant, was Chase Clayton's discarded, suicidal lover.

And he refused to dwell on worst-case scenarios. Josephine Ellen Whitford, twenty-five years old, from Riverfork—all information they'd learned from her driver's license—was going to be okay. She had seemed dazed, scraped and bruised and maybe concussed, but surely not damaged enough to be in danger.

Whatever mischief she'd come here to start, he would face when it presented itself. If it ever did. He still hoped he might have misunderstood her last, slurred words.

He took a deep breath as he waved the Wilcoxes' car down the drive, which was turning blue in the twilight. He shut his eyes for a minute, gathering his focus for the next job…probably finding a taxi for old Portia Luxton, who had stopped driving ten years ago.

He could handle it, whatever it was. He'd been through worse things than this. His parents' deaths and the collapse of his first marriage, for starters. And of course the life of a horse breeder came with a hundred little agonies, from the liquid-eyed foals who take a few breaths and die, to the beautiful, doomed stallions whose wild streaks can't be tamed.

"It's going to be all right," Sue said, appearing at his elbow. Her voice was soft. "It'll be the talk of the town for a week or so, and then Elspeth Grimes will see Elvis in the oil stains on her garage floor and everyone will move on."

"I know." He appreciated Sue's common-sense approach to things, which had been her trademark, even as a child. It was the main reason he'd agreed to this marriage. He could trust her to keep it clean. To carry their plan out to the letter. Marry him, satisfy her autocratic grandfather's absurd will, then take the money and run.

No sticky emotional swamps. No tangles, no hidden agenda.

No last-minute complications, like sex. Or love.

"I know," he said again. "I'm just sorry it spoiled your party."

"It didn't." She smiled, but her mouth and her eyes didn't match. She looked toward the house. "I hope she's okay. She looked kind of…sick, don't you think? I mean, not just hurt from the accident, but unwell."

Chase nodded. He had thought exactly that. Miss Whitford didn't look like a healthy woman. She was painfully thin, and so pale she might have been made of wax. She probably had beautiful eyes when she was rested, large and blue, with feathery black lashes. But right now they were dull, sunken into deep circles like river stones set in mud.

"I wonder who she is." Susannah was still looking at the house.

Again, Chase merely nodded, trying to hide how much he, too, wanted the answer to that question. Susannah had no idea that the woman had spoken both their names and had even said she wanted to stop the wedding. He wasn't planning to talk about those cryptic, disturbing words. Not until he had to.

But for the love of God, what could the woman's motives be? No one had a problem with this wedding. No one wanted to stop it.

Everyone in Texas knew that Susannah Everly had inherited a raw deal from her grandfather, who had written his will while under the influence of alcohol, the leading edge of Alzheimer's and one of his all-too-common rages.

It was only fitting, their neighbors believed, that her best childhood pal should help her out of it. A few romantics even dreamed that a butterfly of love might come winging out of the chrysalis of friendship, creating that storybook happy ending everyone craved.

No. No one wanted to stop this wedding. Not even Trent Maxwell. That's how much the poor sucker loved her.

"Here comes Dr. Marchant," Sue said. She put her hand on Chase's arm. He glanced at her steady profile, and he wondered if she'd heard the rumors. What a mess. He remembered promising Trent, just an hour ago, that he'd never embarrass her.

He wondered how long he could keep that promise. Perhaps no longer than it took a seventy-year-old man to travel the few yards of oyster-shell driveway between them and the house.

He watched the old man striding toward them, his shock of leonine white hair glowing, even in this gathering gloaming. His face was unreadable in the dim light, but he'd taken off his jacket and rolled up the sleeves of his white dress shirt. Something in his movements suggested that his news would not be good.

When Marchant reached them, he didn't waste time with a preamble. He had always given his diagnoses the same way he gave his medicines—nothing more than you needed, and nothing less. And he expected you to take it like a man, even if you were only four and frightened.

He didn't believe in sugarcoating.

"She's going to be fine," he said.

"Oh, thank heaven," Sue breathed. She squeezed Chase's forearm.

Chase knew Marchant's expressions better than Sue. He knew there were more pills here to swallow. "But?"

"The girl is a Type I diabetic," the doctor

said, looking grim. "She hasn't eaten since this morning, and apparently she vomited that up hours ago. She was very nearly in insulin shock. It's amazing she could still drive at all."

"Good grief," Chase said. "I knew it was something, but I wouldn't ever have thought of that." He watched the older man carefully. "Is that all?"

"No." Marchant glanced toward Susannah. "Maybe we should talk privately?"

Sue's hand was very still on Chase's arm. He could feel the slight tremor that ran through her index finger. "Of course," she said in an even voice. "Whatever you prefer."

"No," Chase said. "I don't have any secrets from Sue, Matt. Whatever it is, tell us both."

Marchant shrugged. "Okay. Ms. Whitford is generally in very poor condition. Recent weight loss, maybe a little anemic. I'd say she's overworked, underfed and possibly depressed."

He hesitated, an uncharacteristic move. It

chilled Chase to the bone. Whatever came next, Marchant *really* didn't want to say it.

"The bottom line is, the girl is pregnant."

Sue's hand dropped. "Oh, my God," she breathed. She looked at Chase. "Pregnant?"

Chase looked at her, and he shook his head. "No." He turned to Marchant and shook his head again. "No."

"I'm afraid so," the doctor said, looking first at Chase, then at Susannah, and then back at Chase. For the first time, his dark intelligent eyes showed his age. "I confirmed it, of course, before I agreed to speak to you at all. She is indeed with child. I'd say about three months gone."

"And…" Chase couldn't finish the sentence. He shifted his feet to find firmer ground, and then he tried again. "And—"

"And I'm sorry, son. She says that you're the father."

JOSIE WRAPPED HER PALMS around the cool glass of orange juice brought to her by a uniformed maid moments ago. She used both hands, because she still felt a little shaky, even though the doctor had assured her that the injection he'd given her should stabilize her blood sugar just fine.

She leaned her head back against the cool sheets and shut her eyes. She must have been pretty far gone this time. She'd had insulin reactions before, of course. They had been a part of her life for two decades, since she was diagnosed at only five years old.

But this one had been the worst ever. The doctor had told her about the crash, though she remembered nothing after she took that last left turn, steering her car under the arching iron sign that said Clayton Creek Ranch.

He said she was lucky, given how fast she was going, to escape with only some cuts and abrasions. But she didn't feel lucky. She hurt everywhere. And she knew the car was totaled. It probably didn't look like much to a rich doctor, but it had meant the world to her.

It had meant she could get to work, at least. And to the clinic.

Now what would she do?

Especially if, as she feared, Chase refused—

She heard footsteps coming down the hall, and her hands flew to her hair, trying to smooth the tangles. She caught a glimpse of herself in the dresser mirror, and forced them down again.

What was the use? Her hair had lost the shine he used to admire. It wouldn't spill like honey through his fingers anymore. She'd lost ten pounds, in all the wrong places. She'd cried off her mascara and worried away any hint of lipstick long before she got to the ranch. And now she had a bandage on her forehead and a black eye that made her resemble an off-kilter raccoon.

Chase had turned his back on her two months ago, when she'd been pink-cheeked and bright-eyed with first love. His lust wasn't likely to be reawakened by her "beauty" today.

She'd have to appeal to his honor, or nothing at all.

Which was why her hands started to tremble again as the footsteps drew closer. This was a man who hadn't even bothered to leave a goodbye note. Honor probably wasn't his strong point.

She forced herself to watch the door steadily. She squared her shoulders, trying to look as dignified as possible. She didn't need to cower before him. She hadn't created this baby alone. They had done it together, with laughter and tenderness and passion, however short-lived it had been.

She might be a poor waitress, and he might be a rich rancher. But this was the twenty-first century, and she had no intention of slinking away to starve nobly on the streets for her sins. She wasn't a martyr or a fool.

They'd made the baby together, and they would face the consequences together. She lifted her chin and waited for him to show up in the doorway.

But the man who appeared there wasn't

Chase. He was older, for one thing. Short and neat, brunette and sober-faced.

"Hello, Ms. Whitford," he said. "I'm Chase Clayton's lawyer. May I come in?"

"His lawyer?" She felt some of the bravado whoosh out of her, as if a hole had been torn in her sail. So far she'd seen Chase's doctor, his maid, and now his lawyer. Apparently he had an army of people he could send ahead, like the military's front lines, to wear the enemy down.

"Yes. Jim Stilling. May I come in?"

She nodded. "Of course, Mr. Stilling. It isn't my room. I'm not in a position to deny anyone access to it."

He smiled, waving that idea away and entered the room. He sat on one of the soft chairs, which were covered in butter-colored silk. He looked at home there, even though the decor was so feminine, with powder-blue and butter-yellow-flowered wallpaper, a white lace canopy on the bed and a huge window overlooking rolling green hills.

She'd never slept in a room this beautiful, much less owned one. She'd been trying not to let that intimidate her.

"And please," he said, still smiling softly. "Call me Jim. So. Are you feeling better?"

Josie knew a lot of lawyers. The Not Guilty Café was full of them. Her stepfather was a lawyer, too. But she'd never met one with such warm eyes and gentle smile.

All the better to fool you with, my dear.

"Yes," she said politely. "Much better."

"Good. I'd like to talk to you a minute, if you don't mind. Dr. Marchant has told me about your condition. Apparently you gave him permission to discuss it?"

She flushed slightly, remembering. She'd told the doctor he could shout the news to the whole world if he wanted. She had been angry, embarrassed that she'd caused such a ruckus, ashamed of her scrawny, scraped-up body, which she'd been required to lay bare for his inspection, so that she could prove she wasn't lying about the baby.

"Yes," she said. "He has my permission.

The pregnancy isn't something I'll be able to keep secret very long, anyhow."

The lawyer steepled his fingers. "And is it your contention that Chase Clayton IV is the father of this child?"

Her eyes narrowed. That sounded like something on a subpoena.

"Maybe we should dispense with this prologue, Mr. Stilling, and get to the point." She drew herself up even straighter in the bed. She put her hands under the blanket, to hide the tremor that hadn't quite disappeared. She didn't want to appear weak. She was tired of being weak. Now that she knew why she had been feeling so sick and exhausted lately, she wasn't afraid anymore.

And she was all through with cringing and enduring. She was going to be a mother, and that was a job that called for courage. It was time to find out if she had some.

"Yes," she said. "It is officially, legally, my contention that Chase Clayton IV is the father of my baby. Is it his contention that he is *not*?"

"I didn't say that," the man said, shaking

his head as if alarmed by her sudden adamance. "I haven't spoken to Chase about this yet. I assume Dr. Marchant is filling him in on the situation at this very moment. He doesn't know I'm here. In fact, I probably shouldn't be here. It's just that, I'm very fond of Chase, and I thought perhaps I might—"

"Make me go away? Make me change my story? That isn't going to happen, Mr. Stilling. Back in January, Chase and I spent a month as lovers. He may regret that now. In fact, given that he's planning to marry someone else, I'm fairly sure he does. But regret doesn't change the fact that it happened. It also doesn't change the fact that I'm carrying his child."

"There's no need to upset yourself, Miss Whitford. I'm not trying to make you do anything. It's just that…" Stilling looked sincerely uncomfortable. "You see, I've known Chase a long time, and it's hard for me to believe that—"

"Chase is the father," she said firmly. "I understand that you know nothing about me, about my character. Maybe you think that…I don't know, that I have dozens of lovers, and I just picked the richest one to pin it on."

The lawyer shook his head. "No. Really. I'm not implying anything of the sort."

But he was thinking it. Of course he was. It would be the perfect out for Chase, if he could prove she was a tramp. This Stilling guy was a lawyer, and he represented a rich man accustomed to taking what he wanted and throwing it away when he was through.

Like her stepfather. Funny, how that seemed to be her pattern. Her mother's husband had forced her out of the house at eighteen. For her own good, he said. So that she'd learn to stand on her own two feet. A year later, in a moment of weakness, she'd asked him if she could move back home for a while, just until she got her AA. He was drunk, of course, but his answer was unequivocal. Hell, no. Having her show up again was the equivalent of having the trash guy bring back his garbage.

As if the insult had happened yester-day, she felt tears pressing at the back of her eyes, and she fought them away. They were part of the old weakness, and she was done with them.

"I know what you're thinking," she said. "But it simply isn't true. I have had only one lover. It was Chase. I met him at the restaurant where I work, and he was—"

Somehow she stopped herself. She didn't need to justify herself to this man. She wasn't on trial for immorality here. She didn't have to tell him how lonely she'd been, and how the handsome cowboy had swept her off her feet, which were aching like fire from twelve-hour shifts. She didn't have to admit how easily he'd romanced her with a fancy car, expensive meals and whispers about the stars in her eyes and the honey in her hair.

That story wouldn't make her look one bit better. It would make her look gullible and pathetic, which was worse than trashy any day.

And anyway, how could she ever describe how sweet Chase had seemed, at the beginning? The first night, after they'd made love, they had stayed up for hours, eating the chocolates he'd brought her and telling each other stories about their childhoods.

The sex had been nice, but it was those stories that had made her fall in love with him. She'd been able to picture him as a little boy of eight, fishing in the creek that bore his name and throwing everything back. And at nine, killing a rattlesnake with a golf club and shaking for an hour afterward.

She'd never known a man so willing to admit he had a tender heart.

"Anyhow, it's all true," she said. "We spent a month together. Every day. I know all about him, Mr. Stilling. I know he got his first horse when he was fourteen, and its name was Captain Kirk. I know that when he was ten his collie died, and he carved the gravestone himself."

The lawyer's eyes widened slightly.

"The doctor says I can't get out of bed, but if I could, I'd go to that window, and I bet I could see the stone from here. It says Yipster, the World's Nicest Dog."

"Anyone could know those things," he said carefully. "Anyone could—"

"No," a harsh voice from the doorway said. "Not anyone."

Stilling leaned forward. "Chase!"

The man in the doorway didn't take his gaze from Josie. "Only someone who knew me well could have told you those stories, Miss Whitford, and I'd like to know who it was."

She shook her head, feeling nauseated again. She wondered if her blood sugar might have dipped again, from all the stress. She couldn't quite follow what seemed to be happening. Who was this? Were they trying to fool her, bringing in someone to pose as Chase and hope she'd snap at the bait?

The man glaring in at her was very tall and beyond handsome, with thick golden hair and the bluest eyes she'd ever seen. They were also the coldest eyes she'd ever seen.

"It was Chase who told me," she began, her voice betraying her anxiety. It was like walking on a road rigged with land mines. She didn't know what they were trying to do.

"No," the man said roughly. "That's a lie."

A woman stood at his elbow, just behind

him. She looked familiar, though Josie had no idea why. "Chase," the woman said gently. "That's too harsh."

"It's not harsh—it's true. You are lying, Miss Whitford. I told you nothing. Until you wrecked your car in my driveway this afternoon, I had never seen you before in my life."

Dr. Marchant's low, gruff voice came from the hall, somewhere out of sight. "Chase, really."

Josie tilted her head back, trying to make enough room in her lungs to breathe. Thank God she wasn't standing up. She would have fallen into a heap, like a puppet with no strings.

"Well? I'm waiting for an explanation, Miss Whitford. I swear on my life, I have never seen you before."

He sounded…so certain. So indignant.

So exactly how an honest man unjustly accused would sound.

The bed seemed to tilt. Her heart hitched.

But then everything cleared. And suddenly she understood.

Yes, she thought as she took in the man's generous mouth, his wide, clear brow and his intelligent eyes, everything finally made sense. The one mystery, the one thing she hadn't ever been able to figure out, came clear. She'd never understood how a boy who had cried over killing a rattlesnake could grow into a man who could break a woman's heart without batting an eye.

How could anyone change so much?

He couldn't. That was the simple, terrifying answer.

He hadn't *changed*. The dashing heartbreaker she'd met, and the tenderhearted rancher's son whose stories had won her heart…they were two different men entirely.

"Damn it, woman. Say something."

She met his furious gaze helplessly. She had nothing to say. Not to him. All she could possibly say was…

"I'm so sorry, Mr. Clayton. I've never seen you, either."

CHAPTER FOUR

IT TOOK SEVERAL MINUTES for Chase to clear the room. Obviously, once Josie had dropped her bomb, no one wanted to leave before the mystery was sorted out.

The lawyer, in particular, resisted. He used euphemisms, but Josie wasn't an idiot, so she understood. He was trying to warn Chase about being alone in a bedroom with a woman like her. According to Stilling, Josie probably planned to wait thirty seconds, scream "Rape!" and live off the hush money for the rest of her life.

But apparently no one ordered Chase around in his own house, even for his own good. Though he never once raised his voice, pretty soon everyone was filing out, slowly and still chattering, offering last-minute advice.

Everyone except the woman Josie had seen earlier, standing just behind Chase in the doorway. As soon as the auburn-haired beauty entered the room, Josie recognized her. She was Susannah Everly, Chase Clayton's fiancée. Apparently she was going to be the official witness.

Josie wondered whether Susannah was staying to protect Chase from the crazy lady in the bed, or to protect her own romantic interests. Either way, Josie could imagine how much the woman must resent an interloper on a day like this. Josie had already gathered that she had crashed an engagement party...*literally*.

"Okay, Ms. Whitford," Chase said, his voice hard. "Let's talk."

Josie braided her fingers in her lap, hoping that would keep them from feeling so shaky. "I wish I knew what to say. Obviously someone's been impersonating you, Mr. Clayton, and I fell for it. I was upset this morning, when I set out to come here. I'd just learned I was pregnant, and I...I didn't think it through, I suppose."

She looked at him, trying to believe what seemed to be true—that he was the real Chase Clayton. "It was terrible timing. I'd say I'm sorry for causing such a commotion, but that doesn't seem to quite cover it, does it?"

"No," he agreed. "Not even close."

She waited, unsure where to go from here. On the exhausting drive to this ranch, she'd been fueled by fiery indignation, believing she must make Chase do right by his own child. But now...

Now she just felt like a fool.

Chase was watching her through narrowed, appraising eyes. She lifted her chin. Okay, she had been a fool, but she didn't have to be a *pitiful* fool. If only she were sure her legs would hold her, she'd get out of the bed and...

And what? Her car was in bad shape. And she certainly didn't have money to take a cab all the way back to Riverfork.

"I think maybe you'd better start from the beginning," he said slowly. "For starters, how did you meet this…this man you thought was me?"

"About three months ago, he came into our café, the Not Guilty Café in Riverfork. I wait tables there every morning."

She almost added that she went to school in the afternoons, that she was just one semester away from getting her associate's degree, but she bit her lip. He hadn't asked for her life story. And besides, she wasn't ashamed of being a waitress. She didn't have to impress this man or his elegant fiancée.

She noticed that Susannah had subtly separated herself from the conversation. The tall, slender woman stood over by the window, silhouetted against the deep blue, dying light. Of course she could still hear every word, but Josie appreciated the tact. At least Josie didn't have to look into her eyes while she revealed her own stupidity.

She turned back to Chase. "He came in every day for a week before he ever asked me out. He always requested one of my tables. He was friendly. We talked a lot. He said his name was Chase Clayton IV. He told me all about his life, his ranch, his—" She stopped. "I guess it was your life, though. Your ranch."

"Apparently. But you just swallowed the story whole? You didn't check him out? You didn't even ask for identification?"

"No. It never occurred to me. Some things you just take for granted, don't you? You can't go around suspecting everyone of fraud. Do you check out every single person you meet?"

"Absolutely. Especially if it involves business, or anyone who will be granted…a degree of intimacy." He took a step closer. "Like sleeping in my guest room, for instance. Stilling is downstairs doing a Lex-isNexis search on you right now. If you have a criminal background, he'll find it. And if you do, then believe me, Miss Whitford, you'll be out of that bed in a hurry."

She frowned, stung by his tone. "And you can believe *me*, Mr. Clayton, that I have no intention of being your *guest* one second longer than is absolutely necessary."

She felt herself flushing. "I'm not sure what you suspect me of, Mr. Clayton. I've already admitted, in front of witnesses, that I made a mistake. That I'm not accusing you of being the man who…the man I…"

Over by the window, Susannah stirred. "Chase, Dr. Marchant said she needed to rest. Don't you think…" She let the sentence dwindle off.

Chase looked at her for a minute. Then he took a deep breath. "Yeah, you're right, Sue." He rubbed his hand across the back of his neck, mussing the golden waves of hair that curled around his collar. "You're right, darn it. You always are."

He smiled. It was just a one-sided, self-mocking smile, and it wasn't even directed at Josie, but it was enough to make the soles of her feet tingle under the covers. *Wow.* She could only imagine the sex appeal if both sides were in play.

Susannah Everly was a very lucky woman. But then Josie had known that from the moment she glimpsed the woman's beaming face in the paper.

Chase turned back toward the bed. "I'm sorry, Miss Whitford. I'm being a jerk. If my mother were alive, she'd tan my hide. You are my guest, and I'm not doing a very good job of being a host. And honestly, I don't always see a conspiracy behind every shrub. It's just that—"

"I know. I embarrassed you in front of your guests. I'm very sorry. Your reputation—"

He waved his hand. "I don't give a damn what the guests think. Most of them are my friends, and they'll understand. The rest of them don't matter. And, just for the record, the only reputation that matters around here belongs to my horses."

"Yes, your quarter horses. They're considered the best in Texas. Especially Alcatraz, right? And you almost didn't buy him, which would have been a terrible mistake. His stud fees alone—"

"*Damn!* He knew everything about me, didn't he?" He narrowed his eyes. "Who *is* this guy? What can you tell me about him? Did he look like me?"

She gazed at him. "No."

"What did he look like? Tell me everything you remember. If he knew me that well, I might recognize him."

She hardly knew where to begin. Looking at this man, trying to think of him as Chase, was as disorienting as looking into a fun house mirror.

Her Chase had been handsome, with a slight, but well-muscled body and a face so pretty it was almost feminine. The day he sauntered into the café, his rosebud lips and china-blue eyes had turned every female head. He was a little girl's childhood dream come to life, a fairy-tale prince with a charmingly cocked Stetson hat and sexy snakeskin boots.

This Chase wasn't anything that simple. He was too ruggedly male, too intimidatingly *real*, to have stepped out of any kind of dream. He was a good six inches taller than her Chase, with double the shoulder span. His whole body seemed to have been carved from a much-harder material, and his energy radiated out, creating a force field that she imagined few could resist.

His face was full of fascinating contradictions. His square, don't-mess-with-me jaw came to a sweetly dimpled chin. His bedroom-blue eyes were fringed in black lashes so long that when he shut them they brushed the prominent, knife-blade cheekbones below.

His upper lip came to a sharp bow. Not like her Chase's lips. This mouth wouldn't ever make a woman think of rosebuds, because she'd be too busy thinking of… other things.

"He was smaller," she said, though she knew it was woefully inadequate. "Several inches shorter, and…more wiry all over. He had blond hair and blue eyes, but paler than yours. Less intense."

"Was he my age?"

"He said he was thirty-one. He looked about that, I'd say. But again, I didn't check his ID."

"That could be a million guys in Texas alone, including me. Is there anything else that might help? Did he have an accent? Any scars? Tattoos? Injuries? Anything unique?"

She thought hard. It was strange, but her mental image of Chase—her Chase—had grown fuzzy, like someone seen through a fog. What had done that, she wondered? The discovery that he was not merely a garden-variety love-'em-and-leave-'em heartbreaker, but also a first-class fraud and a liar?

Or had he just been obscured by the sheer force of the real Chase?

"Well…he had a slight Texas accent, a nice voice, well-educated East Texas. But that could have been fake, too, I suppose."

"What else?"

She shut her eyes and tried to summon up a clear image. "Nothing else, really. Nothing unique, anyhow."

"There must have been something special about him." Chase sounded impatient. "You met him only three months ago. Dr. Marchant says you're almost three months pregnant. So I repeat. There must have been something special about him."

"Chase." Susannah left the window and came toward the bed. "I don't think this is the time to—"

"It's all right," Josie said. She squared her shoulders and looked at Chase. "I don't mind the question. It wasn't that simple, Mr. Clayton. I didn't fall for him because of the way he looked. It was the way he acted. It was the way he made me feel. He was nice to me. He was friendly and had a good sense of humor, and he knew how to have fun. He took me out to expensive dinners, and he listened to me when I talked. He rubbed my feet when they hurt after work, and he bought me things. Not flowers and perfumes, but things I needed. A teapot. A clock radio. New sheets."

Susannah moved even closer, her hand outstretched. "Miss Whitford, you're very tired. It's been a terrible day—"

"No," Josie broke in. She didn't want pity. Especially not from this woman, who had everything Josie would never have— a healthy, golden life with the real Chase, the sexy rancher with gentle hands and a tender heart.

She hadn't told them how the fake Chase had really seduced her—using the sweet, corny stories of a little boy who loved his home, his horse and his dog. The little boy who sold a baseball card to buy his mother chocolates, but ate them all before he made it home.

She had believed her heart—and her body—were safe in the hands of a man like that.

She tried to speak. To her horror, she realized she'd begun to choke up again.

"I'm sorry," she said, clearing her throat. "I'm all right. I think being pregnant does a number on your hormones, that's all. I'm not crying. At least not...not because of Chase."

Chase gazed at her, unblinking. "I'm Chase."

"Of course." She wiped roughly under her eyes with the knuckles of her index fingers. "You know what I mean. I'm not crying because of him. I'm anxious about the future, and of course the baby. And

I'm shocked to discover how completely I was conned. But I'm not heartbroken."

"Why not? Are you saying that what you felt for him wasn't really love?"

She hesitated. That first week, she had thought it might be. But maybe it had just been…hope.

Hope that she could still be lighthearted and happy, in spite of working so hard and worrying every minute about money.

Hope that, on any given day, something special just might walk through that café door and single her out. *Her.* Sickly little Josie Whitford.

Now she had new hope. Hope that she could stay healthy enough to have a healthy baby. Hope that she could be a good mother. Hope that she could face her future, whatever it was, with courage.

And honesty.

She took a deep breath. She might as well begin today.

"No," she said, in spite of how she knew it would sound. "It definitely wasn't love."

"WHAT A MESS." Susannah Everly tossed her front door keys onto the end table and dropped her purse on the floor. Shutting her eyes, she leaned back against the foyer wall. "What a big, bad, supersized Texas mess."

"Yeah, I heard."

Susannah's eyes flew open. She hadn't realized that Nicole was within earshot. She'd sent her little sister home with the Parkers hours ago, with instructions to clean her room and do her homework. Judging from how Nikki's room had looked this morning, that should have taken her a couple of weeks.

Where was she? Susannah scanned the foyer, which was large and beautiful, the prettiest foyer of any ranch in the county. Her mother had decorated this foyer right before she died. Susannah had been fifteen at the time—Nikki a toddler. Susannah had been allowed to pick out the paneling, and she'd chosen a honey pine that she still loved just as much today.

Of course, she loved every inch of Everly Ranch, which had been in her family for six generations. Every hole in the knotty pine floor, every beam and timber and pane of glass. Every leaf on every peach tree in the thousand-acre orchard.

Finally, Susannah spotted Nikki lying at the foot of the staircase, her brown hair fanned out on the floor, just a shade redder than the wood. Her feet were cocked up on the third tread, the cordless phone resting on her stomach. It was her favorite position for a long chat with…

Probably with Eli. The new ranch boy over at the Double C had been spending a lot of time over here, in spite of Susannah's objections that he was too old for Nikki. It was the new hot spot between Susannah and her sister. Just mention the name Eli Breslin, and things got ugly in a hurry.

Right now she ignored the sight of the phone. She wasn't up to swimming in that swamp tonight.

"Yeah," Nikki repeated, a little louder. "I heard."

Susannah straightened. "You heard what?"

Nicole gave her an *oh-brother* look.

"Heard about your super-sized mess." She kicked her bare feet and began using her toes to play with the banister. She knew that irritated Susannah, who actually cared how hard the servants worked.

Nikki had also changed into her tightest cutoff shorts, also guaranteed to annoy. The cream-lace dress she'd worn to the party was probably on a heap in her closet, right above a mildewing swimsuit or stinky sneakers.

"Yep," Nikki continued when she didn't get a rise out of Susannah on the first try. "A real mess. *Everybody's* talking about it."

"Everybody? That's probably a bit of an exaggeration, don't you think? I'll bet there are Bedouins in the Sahara who haven't a clue."

Susannah leaned toward the mirror over the end table and pretended to check her lipstick, although she'd chewed it off hours ago, back in Chase's guest room.

"And speaking of messes, if I went upstairs right now and looked in your room, what would I find?"

She could see, even in the mirror, the glower that passed across Nikki's face. She bit back a sigh. Teenagers were so…melodramatic. And the last thing she needed today was more melodrama.

Nikki swung her feet around and sat up, balancing the phone on one knee. "You're unbelievable, you know that? Your engagement is falling apart, you're the laughing stock of the whole county, and all you can worry about is my room?"

"Don't be absurd. My engagement is not falling apart."

"Oh, yeah? That's not what I hear." Nikki climbed to her feet. Her face was bright and feverish, as if she'd worked herself into a real state.

Susannah turned around, more disturbed than she wanted to let on. "What do you hear?"

"I hear that woman in the accident today was Chase's secret lover. I hear she was trying to commit suicide because Chase was planning to marry you."

Susannah's stomach tightened. "Is that what Eli Breslin told you?"

Nikki scowled. "He's not the only one saying it. You should have seen the Parkers, when they drove me home. They kept looking at each other in this totally shocked way. And then they'd look at me like, poor little kid, she doesn't even know what's going on."

"I think you're imagining things, Nikki. The woman in the crash today is just an old friend of Chase's. She was coming to see him, but she's a diabetic, and she had gone into insulin shock. That's why she lost control of her car."

This was the story she and Chase had agreed on, after they'd left Josie Whitford, pale-faced and frightened, lying in the guest room. As much truth as possible, they'd decided. Not a word of the impostor Chase. It was quite possible, judging from his intimate knowledge of Chase's history, that he was someone from around here, and they didn't want to tip him off. Of course, there still was a possibility that the "fake" Chase had been fabricated by Josie Whitford to advance some agenda they didn't yet understand. Susannah felt sorry for the young woman, but she wasn't buying her story wholesale. She still had some serious reservations.

Apparently Nikki did, too. She'd scrunched up her nose and mouth. "A diabetic old friend?" She snorted. "Do you expect me to believe that?"

All in all, it was a pretty good story. Still, she might have liked to try it out for the first time on a less cynical audience.

Nikki had scrunched up her nose and mouth. She looked very young when she did that, though of course she'd have died if anyone pointed that out.

She snorted. "A diabetic old friend? Do you expect me to believe that?"

"I don't care what you believe." Susannah shrugged. "If you prefer to invent lurid fantasies, that's your choice. All I ask is that you not bore me with them.

I've got to make some calls for the Burn Center tonight, and I'm tired."

With a curse, Nikki tossed the phone toward its regular table, but she missed. The plastic went clattering to the floor.

"God, you really don't give a damn about him, do you? I know you told me it was just a business deal really, whatever *that* means. Personally, I think it's disgusting. You shouldn't marry a man you don't have one single feeling for."

Susannah drew her brows together. "Nikki, that's out of line. You know I care deeply about Chase."

"Care deeply?" Nikki snorted. "I *care deeply* about my iPod. That's not how you describe the man you're going to *marry*. Eli says you just want the Clayton money. He's right, isn't he? You wouldn't care if Chase had a hundred secret lovers, would you?"

Her tone was poisonous, even more insulting than usual. Susannah felt the blood drain from her face. Nikki had always been a handful, even as a toddler. She'd seemed older than her years, more precocious and demanding than such a little girl should be. Certainly more than Susannah, who had been forced into surrogate "motherhood," much too early, knew how to control.

Susannah had always suspected that, behind Nikki's brash facade, lay a painful insecurity. It made sense. Whether it was fair or not. Nikki probably felt abandoned by their parents, who had died together in a car crash so long ago she hadn't had a chance to know them. So yeah, Susannah understood. She even ached for her stormy little sister, who didn't have the memories Susannah had to sustain her.

She just hadn't known what to do about it.

Maybe, she thought, looking at Nikki now, she had made a mistake, not fully explaining why she and Chase had agreed to a marriage of convenience. She couldn't just gloss things over anymore, the way she'd done when Nikki was a child. Maybe, at sixteen going on forty, Nikki was old enough to handle all the facts.

"Sit down," Susannah said.

Nikki looked wary. "Why? I don't want to hear another lecture about Eli."

Susannah moved wearily to the staircase, with its beautiful scrolled banister. She lowered herself onto the nearest tread.

"Not Eli, Nik. I want to explain about Chase. And I'm too tired to stand up while I do it."

Nikki hesitated, but her curiosity overcame her defiance. She plopped down next to Susannah with a heavy sigh. "Okay. Go ahead. Tell me how wrong I am."

"You're not wrong." Susannah leaned back on her elbows, too tired to care what happened to her expensive party dress. "Chase and I aren't in love, not the way you mean. We're very good friends—the best. We always have been, ever since we were kids. You know what a super guy he is."

Nikki shrugged noncommittally, which made Susannah smile. Nikki adored Chase, and everyone knew it. He was the only person on earth she confided in.

"Anyhow, the bottom line is that, because of some weird rules that Grandfather put in his will, I have to get married in order to have any real control of the ranch. And I need control. We're having money problems. You knew that, right?"

"Of course. How could anyone not know, the way you always go on about it? What I don't know is how come. The ranch is huge. And our peaches are like the best anywhere. I don't know anybody who buys anything else."

Susannah thought of all the planning, fretting, investing and pure backbreaking work that went into creating those lush peaches everyone wanted in their pretty cut-glass dessert bowls. But she'd always spared Nikki the details, trying to allow her to grow up carefree, without the worries and obligations that had weighed Susannah down too soon.

Maybe that had been a mistake, too. Maybe a little responsibility would have been good for her.

Well, better late than never.

"It's a combination of a lot of things, Nik. We've had frost two years running. That hurt us a lot. And some of the acres on the west ridge are just about used up. They'll have to lie dormant for a few years before they can be replanted. Worst of all, though, is that one of our best buyers is in deep financial trouble. They just might go bankrupt."

"So? Can't you find another buyer?"

"Believe me, I'm trying. But it's not that easy. There's a lot of competition. The thing is, we've crunched the numbers every way we can think of, and the only answer is to sell some of the land."

Nikki's mouth hung open. "Sell Everly?"

Susannah put her hand on Nikki's arm. "Not the whole ranch, honey. Everly has always belonged to the Everlys, and it always will. Just a couple of hundred acres, not enough to miss really. But enough to put us back in the black."

Nikki rubbed the pad of her thumb over the glossy pink polish on her index finger. Susannah knew that habit. It meant Nikki was thinking hard.

She hoped she wasn't overloading her with too much scary information. There was a mighty fine line between character-building and spirit-crushing.

"I guess I still don't understand what this has to do with marrying Chase," Nikki muttered, staring down at her finger. "Grandfather left you the ranch, right? Can't you do whatever you want?"

"Not unless I'm married, and even then my husband gets to make the decisions. You know how Grandfather was. You know how he felt about women."

Nikki looked up with a half smile. "Totally chauvinist? Totally caveman?"

"Yeah, pretty much."

Susannah sighed, remembering the fights, the rip-roaring yell-fests as she tried to keep an ornery ninety-year-old man from running the ranch into the ground. Arlington H. Everly had a true Texas-sized ego. No one told him what to do. But take advice from a woman? "Not unless my wits get up and go prancing in the pepper patch," he'd vowed.

Tragically, toward the end, it had come to that.

"Does Chase know all this stuff?" Nikki's upturned face looked pale, and, although Susannah might be imagining this, she looked a tiny bit older already.

"Yeah. He knows. He's doing me a favor. You can see that I couldn't risk marrying just anyone. They'd get control of the ranch, and…"

She couldn't even finish the thought.

"Anyhow, I trust Chase. After we've been married a year, he can sell the acres we need to unload. Grandfather didn't stipulate how long the marriage had to last beyond that first year. So then we'll end it, and we'll go back to being friends."

She looked down at Nikki, and to her surprise realized that the girl's eyes were glistening in the light from the overhead chandelier.

Susannah felt her heart squeeze. Damn it. She really *had* screwed up. Nikki must actually have hoped that the "marriage of convenience" might turn into more than that.

She must actually have hoped Chase might become her big brother for real.

"Oh, honey, I'm sorry I didn't talk to you about all this sooner—"

"Don't be," Nikki said roughly. She stood, yanked on the hem of her short-shorts, stretching them out just enough to cover the lacy white underwear. "I don't care what you do."

She headed up the stairs. Susannah watched her go helplessly.

"Nikki…"

The girl reached the first landing, then turned furiously, her face set and white. "I'll tell you one thing, though. You tell me I shouldn't hang out with Eli. Well, at least we really love each other."

"Love?" Susannah rose instinctively to her feet. *"Love?"*

"That's right. And you can say what-ever you want about how young I am, or how stupid I am. At least I know *how* to love somebody. So I guess I'm not as stupid as you are."

CHAPTER FIVE

CHASE HAD MADE IT crystal clear. Under no circumstances was Josie to get up before Dr. Marchant came in the morning, checked her out and gave her the green light.

But by nine, she was too restless to stay put a minute longer, even in this comfortable guest suite, a bedroom and bath that together were nearly as big as her whole apartment.

She'd been awake for hours, since the first bout of morning sickness swept through her around dawn. During the night, someone had placed a tray of soda crackers and a pitcher of ice water beside her bed, and by six she felt strong enough to nibble the edge of one of the little saltine squares.

After that, the house had been too full of noise, doors banging and people calling to one another, trucks pulling up in the drive, horses whinnying and phones ringing. The ranch was coming awake for the day.

A few minutes later, the sun woke up, too, and her pretty room filled with clear lime-colored light that danced on mirrors and curlicue silver picture frames, and even on her water glass.

But she remembered her promise and tried to sit still, waiting for the doctor. She pulled one of the chairs up to the window and sat for an hour, just drinking in the beauty of the ranchland. It seemed to stretch out to forever. The hills rolled softly into the distance, going from green to gray to foggy blue.

She'd been right about where the little hand-carved headstone should be. From her window, she could just see it, beneath the sparkleberry tree, which was shedding its starry white flowers all over the collie's grave.

Funny, that one spot of the Clayton Creek Ranch had been as vividly real to her as her own kitchen. Her lover—she no longer found it comfortable to call him

Chase—had described it so perfectly, down to the way the headstone had been set crooked in the grass.

She tried to picture him standing there, staring down at the sweet, silly inscription and thinking, *Yes, I can use this someday. Some brainless bimbo will fall for this like a pile of rocks.*

After that, she'd paced the room for a while, testing out her legs. In spite of a roaring headache and her purpling bruises, she felt stronger today.

Probably because she'd had a good night's sleep. And, for once, her stomach hadn't been required to wake right up and handle the smell of greasy sausage and fat-marbled bacon.

But even the luxury of laziness grew uncomfortable after a while. She was used to being busy. She checked her watch. Nine-thirty. Despite Chase's command, she needed to get going.

She started with her shot—thank goodness she'd had enough presence of mind, after the shock of discovering she was pregnant, to pack a small bag of essentials, including her insulin.

She wouldn't have wanted to do without a change of clothes, either. Yesterday's outfit was ruined. The skirt was torn, and the scoop neckline was newly decorated with a circlet of teardrop-shaped bloodstains.

The guest bathroom was well stocked, so she brushed her teeth and washed her face. She stared at the raccoon-eyed stranger in the mirror, and tried to fluff her hair into some semblance of self-respect. It was hopeless, so she gave up.

When she left her room, she entered a long, wide hallway that smelled like a spring garden. Simple arrangements of hand-picked blooms—from phlox to daffodils—were everywhere, on tables, beside windows, even spilling out of an architectural niche in the wall.

Someone at the Clayton Creek Ranch was passionate about flowers—and she quickly discovered who it was. As she turned the corner toward the staircase, she spotted a short, round woman bending over a vase, clearly searching for the perfect placement of a sprig of bright pink dogwood.

The woman looked up as she heard Josie's footsteps. She was probably about fifty, but she had a baby face, cheeks as pink as the flower and the most cheerful smile Josie had ever seen.

"You must be Miss Whitford! How are you feeling, honey? I'm Imogene. Officially I'm the housekeeper, but in reality I do everything around here. Absolutely everything. You looking for Chase? He's still out on the terrace, ignoring that fine breakfast I cooked him. There's plenty, if you're hungry."

Josie smiled, not sure where to grab the conversation first. "I'm feeling much better, thanks," she said carefully, unsure how much Chase would have told his housekeeper.

"And I am a bit hungry." Josie peered over the banister to the sprawling layout below. "But I'm not sure how to get to the terrace."

Imogene tucked the sprig of dogwood into the vase, gave the arrangement one last fluff, then held out her hand. "Come with me. I'll show you."

She led Josie to a big bay window at the end of the hall. "He's right down there, see? Three cups of coffee, but not one forkful of hash browns. Not even a melon cube. The boy could drive a saint insane."

Josie squinted against the bright morning light. At first she just saw the only trees, green grass and white paddock fences. But then she saw Chase.

"Oh, yes. But how do I get out there?"

Imogene patted her arm. "Easy as pie. The house is just one big C-shaped box. Take the main staircase down, U-turn at the bottom and follow the sunlight. Or the intoxicating smell of my world-famous hash browns."

It really was that easy. Josie didn't stop to look into any of the spacious, flower-filled rooms she passed. She didn't want to risk missing her chance to talk to Chase alone.

He had his back to the doorway, so he didn't see her coming. He seemed engrossed in the newspaper, which was folded in half and resting against his leg, which he'd propped against the wrought-iron trestle table. The table practically buckled with food—hard-boiled eggs, bagels, toast, ham, pastries, fresh melons and berries, and enough coffee and tea and juices to float the whole terrace away down the hill.

But he didn't seem to be eating any of it. His left hand rested absently against a coffee cup that she knew had gone cold long ago.

She stole a minute to look at him, to gather her courage. And to see if, in yesterday's emotional state, she had been imagining his extraordinary good looks.

She hadn't.

His golden hair tumbled freely across his broad forehead, and his chin was dusted with a stubble about two shades darker. He wore faded jeans and soft leather boots, but they were topped by an expensive blue dress shirt that fit his broad shoulders perfectly. An elegant navy blazer with gold buttons lay across the back of another chair.

He wasn't glossed up for a party today, but the real, everyday Chase Clayton was even more attractive.

Half big business, half cowboy. All man. "Mr. Clayton?"

"Do you think you could bring yourself to call me Chase?"

She frowned. "I think that, given our situation…given how you feel about my showing up here—'

"No." He put out a hand. "Look, I need to apologize. I was a jerk yesterday. I was just shocked, that's all. But I shouldn't have been so rough. Please call me Chase? This Mr. Clayton stuff is so formal, given…" He grimaced. "Well, given that you seem to know every dumb thing I ever did in my checkered past."

She nodded. "Of course." She cleared her throat. "Chase."

It felt awkward, though, and her voice cracked.

"Darn it. Don't say it like that. Say it like you mean it." He took a sip of coffee and grimaced, discovering no doubt that it was stone-cold. "It *is* my name, you know. I'll be damned if I'm going to feel like I stole it from him."

"Of course not," she said. *"Chase."*

"That's better. Now, grab some breakfast and tell me what you're doing out of bed. I thought you were going to wait for Marchant."

"I was. But I'm not used to sleeping this late. And if I'm going to make arrangements to get back to Riverfork today…"

His blue eyes widened. "You're planning to go back *today*?"

"If I can, I think I should. You've been very nice, Mr.—I mean, Chase. But I can't take advantage of your hospitality forever."

"One day is hardly forever. And what about your car? I haven't heard from the garage, but I have a feeling your insurance company is going to total it out. You probably don't remember how it looked, having been unconscious at the time, but I do." He smiled. "It was a wreck."

She didn't doubt it. The details were hazy, like images from a nightmare, but she half remembered the smell of gas, and the surreal hissing of steam.

"I'm sure you're right," she agreed.

"They'll never pay to repair it. The car might have been worth five hundred dollars, but only if I'd just filled the gas tank."

He opened his mouth, then closed it again, as if he'd thought better of whatever he'd been about to say. A line appeared between his eyebrows.

"Don't worry," she said quickly. "I'm not hinting that I need a ride all the way back to Riverfork. Though I would appreciate it if you could spare a car to take me to the bus station."

His frown deepened. "The bus station?"

"Yes." He probably wouldn't be caught dead boarding a bus, but she was very glad that she could actually afford to do so. When she first woke up, she'd used the phone in the guest room to call her bank's 800 number and confirm her checking account balance. Then she'd called Greyhound's toll-free line and inquired about the price of a one-way ticket to Riverfork.

The first number was, thank God, slightly larger than the second. She could at least get home on her own steam, and salvage that much of her pride.

After that…

Well, after that things were likely to get a little sticky. With no job and no money, and a fatherless baby on the way…

"Look, Josie." Chase put one foot up on the edge of his chair and leaned his elbow on his knee. "Please get something to eat and sit down. We need to talk."

"About—" She caught herself before she said "Chase." "About the man who used your name?"

"Yes." He grabbed a plate and began piling juicy squares of cantaloupe onto it. "Look, you need to eat. Marchant told me a little about diabetes, and if you've had your insulin, you really need—"

He broke off, frowning. "You have had your insulin, right?"

She smiled at the protective tone, though she knew he was probably only worried she might pass out, bust her head on these pretty Mexican tiles, then file a lawsuit. "Yes. I've had it."

"Good. So first, you eat. Then, we'll talk about—" He handed her the plate and a fork. "You know, we really need to think of something to call this jerk. I've got some colorful ideas, but I don't think Miss Manners would approve of any of them."

She took the chair he held out and, settling the plate on the table, speared one of the pieces of cantaloupe. She did need food, and besides, it looked too good to resist. And Imogene had been right about the hash browns. After two years at the Not Guilty Café, Josie had forgotten that hash browns could smell like fresh onions and crisp peppers instead of day-old backfat.

"How about Fake Chase?" She raised her brows. "That's what I've been using in my head."

"No. No Chase anything. I want a clear distinction between him and me." He poured himself a fresh cup of coffee, then sat back down beside her. "Okay, let's see. How about Mr. Flim Flam?"

She smiled wryly. "That fits, I guess."

"Okay, then." He slapped the table, then leaned back with a satisfied sigh. "Flim Flam it is. Flim for short."

While she applied herself to the fruit, he got another plate and filled it with a couple of eggs, some hash browns and a bagel.

"I can't eat all that," she said, alarmed.

"Try. I'll share it with you. That'll make Imogene deliriously happy."

They ate in silence a few minutes. At some point, she sensed that he was just watching her, so she looked up.

"What?"

Out here, in the morning sunlight, his eyes looked bluer than the sky over his head, and just as clear and steady.

"I'm going to have to find him, Josie. You know that, right?"

Someone was training a horse in the nearest paddock, and she could hear the low nickering, alternating with the trainer's gentle voice. She shut her eyes for a minute, enjoying the peaceful sound.

"Yes," she said. She opened her eyes again and met his gaze calmly. "I don't blame you.

He can't be allowed to go on using your identity for...for his own purposes."

"No. He can't."

"What will you do when you find him? Will he go to jail?"

"Would that bother you?"

She thought a minute. "I don't know. Part of me would like to watch while you string him up by the thumbs." She chewed the final nugget of cantaloupe. "But another part of me..."

"No." He shook his head firmly. "Please don't tell me you still harbor the secret dream of becoming Mrs. Flim Flam."

"Of course not. Even when we first started out, I always knew he wasn't going to stay forever. That wasn't why I came here, you know. I wasn't going to try to force you...him...*anyone*...to marry me."

"Why did you come, then?" He toyed with his coffee, though he hadn't taken his gaze from her. "What made you drive here like a bat out of hell, not even stopping long enough to eat?"

She'd known he'd ask, sooner or later.

Again, she could only be honest, no matter how idiotic it sounded.

"I got sick at work yesterday morning, and so I went to the clinic. I thought I had the flu. I assumed the doctor would give me some pills, and my biggest fear was trying to find the money to fill the prescription. But when he told me that I was pregnant…"

She moved the hash browns around on her plate, her appetite vanishing. It was difficult, even thinking back to yesterday, when the words "you're going to have a baby" had come at her like a wrecking ball, knocking her into a million little pieces.

Luckily, she seemed strong enough today that she didn't choke up every time she tried to explain herself about anything.

"The truth is, I think I just panicked. It was overwhelming. I was terrified. I don't make much money as a waitress—and I've been using every extra penny for my tuition at the community college. But a *baby*…I knew I couldn't manage without help. All I knew was that Chase—"

"Not Chase." He touched her hand, a gentle reminder. "Flim."

"Right." She tried to smile. "Anyhow, all I could think was that Flim had an obligation to this baby. That he couldn't just run away and leave me to deal with it alone."

He hadn't moved his hand, and now he exerted a small pressure. It didn't feel like pity, which she would have hated. It felt like understanding, one human being to another. The warmth was bracing, and Josie realized her fingers were cold, even though the spring morning was mild and sunny.

"That's exactly what I hoped you'd say," he said. "You're right, Josie. He can't just run away. We need to find this guy. Both of us. We may have different reasons, but they amount to the same thing. We both want him to pay for what he's done. I think we should work together."

"Together?"

"Yes. You can stay here a few days, take a little more time to recuperate. We'll see how quickly we can make the insurance company settle up, and that will give us plenty of opportunity to talk it over, narrow down the possibilities. Your boss will okay the sick leave, I'm sure. If he balks, we'll e-mail him a picture of your black eye."

"I don't have a job," she said. "Not since I introduced my manager to the joys of morning sickness. Or rather…my manager's tacky snakeskin boots."

He groaned. "One more sin Flim has to do penance for. We'll make him buy your manager some new boots. The tackiest ones in Texas."

She smiled. "I guess this means I passed your LexisNexis test," she said. "You didn't find a criminal record?"

"Well, there was that speeding ticket two years ago, but I already knew you were a wild woman behind the wheel."

"I was late for work that day," she protested with a laugh. Then she sobered. "More to the point, I guess this means you've decided that Flim actually does exist? That I'm not just here running some complicated con?"

He nodded slowly. "I guess it does. So

what do you say? Will you stay a few days? Shall we pool our resources and find this guy?"

Pool their resources? Hadn't she just made it clear she had none? Wasn't this just charity in disguise? And yet, the idea of staying here a few days, until she felt stronger, until she could decide what to do, was so tempting it scared her.

She could probably pull it off. She could buy a couple of cheap T-shirts to sleep in and a toothbrush. Her only class this term was an online English lit, and he undoubtedly had a computer she could use.

And, of course, she didn't have a job. But rent wasn't due for about three weeks, and she had enough money in savings to cover a few days off.

Maybe even a couple of weeks, if she decided to. Didn't she deserve some time to think things through?

It would be her first vacation in seven years.

He seemed to read her mind. "Say yes, Josie. I could really use your help. You've got the most important resource of all. You're the only one who has seen our friend Flim Flam in the flesh."

She laughed. It really brought the fake Chase down to size, calling him by such a foolish name. A ridiculous name for a ridiculous man who had to snake his way into a woman's bed by pretending to be someone else.

"So?" Chase's eyes sparkled, and he held out his hand. "Do we have a deal?"

"Yes," she said, extending her own. "Thank you, Chase. We have a deal."

DOWN BY GREEN FERN POOL, Clayton Creek bubbled out to form a fifteen-foot-deep swimming hole. In this secret spot, only the brightest afternoon sunbeams were strong enough to muscle their way through the canopy of ancient black gums, sugar maples and loblolly pines.

The air here was always cool and green, crisscrossed with golden shafts of light that, on a good day, speared all the way to the bottom of the crystal clear pool. When the wind blew the trees, little fairy-darts of sun skipped over the water's surface and glimmered on the limestone walls.

Chase rode Captain Kirk slowly along the sandy path beside the creek, partly because the poor old bay wasn't up to anything more energetic, and partly because Chase wanted to savor the scenery.

He'd been coming here since he was a kid, first with his dad and cousins, then as part of the Fugitive Four. Chase, Trent, Susannah and Paul, a group of friends who had believed they were inseparable.

They'd been wrong, of course. At thirteen, fourteen, even just-turned-twenty, how could they have understood life's destructive power? They had no idea that fate sometimes picked you up like a cyclone and dropped you down wherever and whenever it saw fit.

Trent and Chase had made it through okay. And obviously Chase hadn't ever lost Sue. But Trent and Sue, that was a different story. When the cyclone was through, they'd fallen on opposite sides of an ever-widening divide.

And Paul…Paul was gone forever.

Sometimes, all these years later, it was hard to remember exactly what had happened. They'd been so young—only nineteen or so. Chase had just married Lila, a move that was a mistake on many levels. He'd often wondered whether, if he hadn't been distracted by his demanding, glamorous older-woman bride, he could have stopped things from spiraling out of control.

But maybe that was wishful thinking. The only people who could have stopped this tragedy from happening were Trent and Susannah, and they were too tangled up in their own emotional knots to think straight.

They'd been having problems for months. Girls were crazy for Trent—it was just a fact of his good looks and smooth charm. And he liked the attention a little too much. Though Chase knew Trent really loved Sue, Trent hadn't been quite ready to settle into complete monogamy.

The night things fell apart, they were all

at a bar on the outskirts of town, listening to a local band and coaxing Lila, the only one of the group legally old enough to buy beer, to keep the table supplied.

She agreed, probably because the mood was tense as hell. Just two days before, Sue had discovered Trent's one-night-stand with one of their friends from high school—a spoiled cheerleader with curly red hair who hadn't ever taken no as an answer from anybody.

Sue was, understandably, furious. But Sue didn't get mad like normal people. She got even. This time, she obviously decided to hurt Trent by flirting with other men.

Including Paul.

Paul knew what was going on, of course. The Fugitive Four understood each other completely. He knew, just as Chase did, that Sue and Trent were meant for each other. Eventually she would forgive Trent, and things would revert to normal.

So he played along. Maybe too well. After an hour or so, watching Sue and Paul giggle and dance and whisper and touch,

Trent was boiling. Lila thought it was funny, and fed his fury by bringing him beer after beer.

When the tragedy finally happened, it was so fast and strange, Chase could hardly piece it all together later, when they talked to the cops at the hospital. Trent said something to Paul, who said something back, and before anyone realized it wasn't a joke, Trent had loaded up and punched Paul so hard he fell over, taking the table, five beers and a kerosene lamp with him.

The floor was covered in hay, and the fire sprang up so fast it was like a bad dream. Paul lay there burning and screaming. Or maybe it was Susannah who was screaming. Chase and Trent tore off their shirts, and rolled Paul over and over, until there were no more flames. Just the smell of scorched skin, and the sound of people running and hollering and crying.

The ambulance arrived in record time. God knows, the doctors tried.

Paul hung on for cruel, heartbreaking months. But, in the end, he didn't make it.

And neither did Susannah and Trent.

As he reached the swimming hole now, Chase squeezed his eyes, trying to make the tough memories go away. He didn't relive it all that often anymore. He and Trent hadn't talked about it for years. And Sue never did.

He wondered if it might be better, if Sue and Trent *could* talk about it. But it didn't seem likely now. She'd devoted her life to raising money for a local burn center, and to blaming Trent. Trent had devoted his life to showing Sue he didn't give a damn.

What a mess people could make of things!

Still, the swimming hole was a beautiful place, where the best of nature could soothe your soul—and even vanquish your ghosts. Chase had stored up about a million happy memories here.

He should come more often.

Today he was looking for Trent. He'd gone by the manager's office, only to discover that Trent was out getting a water sample from the hole.

Chase saw him now, squatting on one of

the big, flat silver rocks on the east side of the hole. The boat launch, they'd called it, though of course it was too small even for a canoe.

Trent held a plastic bottle in one hand, its screw-on cap in the other. He spotted Chase and waved. "Come on down," he said. "I'm almost done."

Then he dipped his arm in up to the elbow and let the water bubble noisily into the container.

Chase tied up Captain Kirk, who seemed ready for a nap. He'd been tempted to bring one of his younger, spryer horses, but the poor old horse had given him such a longing look he couldn't resist. Besides, the old guy needed the exercise.

He stroked the horse's nose, and Captain Kirk responded with a soft snort and a nudge into his palm. "No treats, buddy." Chase patted his pockets to prove they were empty. "Maybe when we get back."

He made his way carefully down to the swimming hole. The sloping ground around the pool was mossy and covered in ferns, and if you missed your footing you could slide right in.

"Looks pretty good," he said as he got close enough to see the clear water. You could pick out every rainbow-colored rock.

"Yeah," Trent said, still squatting, still staring out into the water. "I think it's okay. You can still see the bottom, and no sign that the vegetation's struggling."

They'd been monitoring the water each week, ever since a developer just upstream from the east branch of the creek had begun grading the site for his new subdivision. A month ago, the man had been cited for a silt containment failure, and Chase was watching him like a hawk. He didn't intend to let anybody degrade his creek.

"Yeah, the water looks good enough to drink. Guess he's worked the kinks out of his containment system?"

Trent stood, shaking the water from his hand. "So far, so good. But I'm going to keep an eye on it anyhow. We're going to send someone out to measure those greenbelts, too. If he doesn't live up to his promises..."

He seemed to register, suddenly, that Chase had come a long way just to stare at a bottle of water. "What're you doing down here, corporal? As I recall, you took in a stray kitten yesterday. Shouldn't you be home giving it milk or something?"

"Yeah." He didn't mind the tone. He'd filled Trent in about his plan over the telephone this morning, and he already knew Trent thought it was a dumb move. "But she's asleep. She's always tired. Marchant says she's anemic, on top of the diabetes. God knows she's as skinny as a rope. The kid must not have been eating right for months."

Trent gave him a straight look. "She's not a kid, Chase. She's grown-up enough to be making babies with somebody."

"I know. That's why I came down here. I need to figure out who that somebody might be. I thought it might be better to do it somewhere we weren't likely to be overheard."

"Imogene listening at keyholes again?"

Chase chuckled, looking around for a dry spot flat enough to sit on. "She doesn't have to. She has supernatural powers. But it's not just Imogene. It's—"

"It's the kitten?" Trent dropped the water sample into a satchel, then arranged himself on a nearby rock. "You don't want her to hear you naming candidates for the World's Biggest Sleazeball award?"

"I don't want *anybody* to hear me."

Trent nodded slowly. "Fair enough. So, where do you want to start?"

That, of course, was the question. And now that they were out here in this peaceful place, Chase found that he didn't want to start anywhere. How was it possible that he knew—and knew *intimately*—anyone who would do such a thing?

He rested his elbows on his knees and stared out at the glimmering pool of glassy blue water. It was gorgeous in the spring. A patch of buttercups at the edge looked like a honey spill in the sunlight. All around the water hole, trees were beginning to flower.

"Look at the old redbud. It's about twice as big now, isn't it?"

Obediently, Trent glanced at the tree, which was covered in rose-purple flowers. "Yeah. But the swamp willow is dead, did you notice? Must have been last year's freeze."

Chase looked across to the south, where the bare willow was standing. "Yeah. Too bad."

With a sigh, Trent scraped his boot across the rock, adjusting his position. "Tell you what, though. If we're going to have a nice long chat about trees, I might need to find a more comfortable rock."

Chase laughed. "Okay, I know, I'm dodging. So here we go. Here's how I see it. Whoever did this has to meet two qualifications. He has to know me well, or know someone who does. And he has to have a serious grudge against me."

Trent smiled. "Not necessarily. He might just think it would be cool to be you for a while. For all you know, it's his form of flattery."

"You don't really believe that. If a guy doesn't want to do something under his own name, he just makes one up. He doesn't stage a charade this elaborate, this risky. He was with her for a month, for God's sake. She might have seen my picture in the paper, or on TV. I'm not exactly invisible. Any day, she might have decided to check him out."

"But she didn't. Maybe he reads people well. I saw her ten seconds, tops, and even I could read *gullible* all over her pretty face."

"Still, it's a risk he didn't have to take. He wanted to take it. He wanted to use my name, my life. Can't you feel the hostility in that? He wanted to prove he was as good as I was—or maybe, in a weird way, that I was as bad as he was."

Trent whistled. "You put it like that, it does sound pretty creepy. Okay, here's a third option. He's certifiably, barking nuts."

"Maybe. But still functioning. Still pretty damn plausible. I've spent a little more time with her than you have, and I know she's not all that gullible. She's more like—" He tried to think of the right word for that look in her eyes. That proud, determined desperation. "More like vulnerable."

If Chase hadn't known Trent so well, he might have missed the slight flicker of pulse in his jaw.

"She's a nice kid, Trent. That's all I'm saying."

"And all I'm saying is that you've got a Sir Galahad complex. You can't save every stray kitten that mews at the door, Chase. I think you've got your hands full already, don't you? Trying to save Sue and all?"

Chase laughed. "Point taken. Although Sue would scratch your eyes out if she heard you say that."

"Sue would scratch my eyes out just for fun. But let's start naming some specific names here before my butt freezes on this rock." He tilted his head. "I assume we both thought of Alexander first?"

"Of course." Alexander was Chase's second cousin, and about ten years ago he'd been caught in Vegas, registered at an expensive hotel as Chase Clayton, drawing money out with Chase's ATM card like water from a tap. They looked a little alike, although Alexander was shorter, his build more boyish.

He was also quite a playboy. When they'd caught him the second night, the two cocktail waitresses with him in the hotel room had burst into tears.

"Let's see if we can find a recent picture to show Josie," Chase said. "And we should find out where he's living these days."

Trent rubbed his chin. "I'm not sure, but I think he's between wives right now, living in San Antonio. Nowhere near Riverfork, but that would make sense. Wouldn't want to foul his own nest. Maybe I'll see if anyone knows where he was a couple of months ago."

"Good. Now, who else? I considered that guy you fired last year, the one who kept harassing the maids. Charming Billy, they called him. But he was too tall, wasn't he? And his grudge would be against you, not me."

"Well, you've fired plenty of people, too, boss."

"Yeah, but I can't remember any who fit this description, can you? About five ten, 180 pounds, blond, slick as hell?"

"Not offhand. But I'll scan the employment records, see if anything jumps out."

"What about people in town?" Chase mentally ran through the vendors, vets, trainers, gardeners, feed stores and cowboys he dealt with every day. A ridiculous number of them seemed to be thirty-something five-tenish blondes.

"How about people I've outbid for horses? And what about that guy who wanted to buy the Hillman land? He seemed to think there was something shady going on, a secret deal or something between me and Hillman. Didn't he make noise about suing?"

Trent nodded. "Yeah. Marx. I dealt mostly with his lawyer, but I saw Marx a few times. He's probably a close-enough fit, so I'll put him on the list. I don't know about the horses, but I can ask around."

He chuckled softly as he picked up a pebble and tossed it into the pond. "Man. Rich guys sure do piss off a lot of people."

"It feels weird, doesn't it, looking at everybody and wondering…do you go around pretending to be me?" Chase shook his head. "Could make you paranoid if you weren't careful."

"Maybe you should ask Sue for ideas, too." Trent stiffened slightly, as he did every time he mentioned her name. "She's been around forever, and she might have the female perspective. I mean, this guy has clearly got some sex appeal, right? You and I might not even see it. Remember how she used to drool over Bucky Sizemore? I thought the guy was a total dweeb, but she said he was hot as a forest fire."

Chase laughed. "She was just pulling your chain, and you know it. Sue never had eyes for anybody but you. If I had a nickel for every hour I spent out here, listening to the two of you talk dirty about the trees…"

In spite of himself, Trent laughed. They both knew it was true. Sue had fallen in love with Trent when she was only about twelve, something that horrified her snobby grandfather. Trent, whose dad had been a science teacher, was the only one of the Fugitive Four who hadn't been a rancher's child. He didn't have his own horse or housekeeper. His family property was marked off in feet, not acres.

But out here, he was king. He was probably the only teenager who had ever wooed a girl with botany. Sue had been hypnotized when Trent told her about the two-winged silverbell with its delicate white flowers and erect stamens that looked like Christmas candles.

She could lie for hours, with her head in Trent's lap, while he told her about the devil's walking stick, the snowflower tree, the ebony blackbeard, the inch plum, the tickletongue.

Chase chuckled, remembering. "You made some of that crap up, didn't you? There's no such thing as the tickletongue."

"Sure there is. Just not necessarily here, in this exact spot." Trent raised one eyebrow. "If I were making it up, do you think I'd call it the *inch* plum?"

Chase grinned. "Guess not. Sorry. I wasn't thinking clearly."

"Nothing new about that." Trent got to his feet. "Come on. This trip down memory lane is officially over. Some of us have work to do."

He picked up his satchel of water samples. Then he paused, squinting. "Hey. How about Bucky Sizemore? He lives over near Big Bend these days. He's blond, isn't he? Not quite six feet."

"Yeah, but he doesn't hate me." When Trent didn't answer right away, Chase frowned. "Does he?"

"Sorry, boss." Trent grinned. "I have a feeling this list is going to be a lot longer than you thought."

CHAPTER SIX

"NO, NO…put the tallest ones in the center." Imogene nudged Josie out of the way and began shifting the long spikes of larkspur in the silver vase. "See? Like this. And be sure to let them breathe. Not too crowded. See?"

"Yes, I see." Josie nodded. "Got it."

That sounded more confident than she actually felt. But since she had begged Imogene for something to do, and this was the chore she'd been given, she didn't want to let the housekeeper down.

When Josie woke up from her nap, she'd come downstairs looking for Chase. But Imogene said he was gone…no one knew exactly where, or when he'd be back. Imogene's hands were busy kneading dough, and she suggested that Josie sit on the front porch and read, in much the same tone she had probably shooed away an annoying little Chase and his collie years ago.

Josie had tried to obey. She'd sat on the wide, white front porch, comfortably ensconced in a wicker settee and watched the wind blow through the bluebonnets.

For about half an hour.

Then she began to fidget. She wasn't a woman of leisure. She was accustomed to working hard all morning, going to school all afternoon, then cramming her homework, housework and errands into evenings that never held enough hours to get it all done.

So, though she hated to be a nuisance, she'd appealed to Imogene. Surely, there must be something she could do. Dishes? Dusting? She'd be glad to take out the trash.

"I think we can find something," Imogene had said finally, slowly nodding, as if she approved of people who wanted to be useful. "There's always work on a ranch."

Josie had wondered if that might mean mucking out a stall, but apparently not. She'd brought her here, to this beautiful wood-paneled library, to create a bouquet of larkspur, baby's breath and fern fronds.

It took about three tries, but finally Josie thought she'd succeeded. She liked flowers, too, and frequently spruced up the arrangements at the café. This one looked good. Mentally, she ticked off the requirements…balance, breathing room, interesting angles, no dead space, a touch of asymmetry to prevent boredom.

Done.

Stretching backward to unkink her spine, she let her gaze wander across the library, which was a large room with a lot of light. She'd been surprised at how elegant the Double C was, both inside and out. She'd expected a lot of antler-rack chandeliers and saddle-shaped bar stools, but, though it was clearly the home of a proud Texan, this ranch had nothing as kitschy as that.

The honey wood paneling kept the room light, and the river rock fireplace rose two stories high, with stones of soothing blue, gray and silver hues. The leather armchairs pulled up to it were dyed a matching blue.

Chase's desk, which dominated the back half of the room, was strong and masculine, but with a hint of grace in its curving lines. A lot like the man himself, she thought.

It was fairly orderly, though he'd left some papers scattered on its surface, which she took as a sign that he expected to come back soon. She wandered over, drawn by a set of framed photographs on the credenza behind the desk.

Was it possible Chase knew Flim Flam well enough to have a picture of him somewhere? She picked up a group shot and scanned the faces. No…these were teenagers. She could identify Chase, and there was Susannah. But the rest were strangers to her.

Another was clearly of his parents—a sad-eyed beauty, filled with quiet elegance, leaned her head onto the shoulder of a larger-than-life, broadly smiling man in a Stetson hat. Josie looked closer. She could see a little of each of them in Chase.

She had just picked up another photograph when she heard the sound of light footsteps in the hall.

"Imogene, come see! I think you'll be proud of your pupil."

"It's not Imogene," a pleasant voice said. And then its owner rounded the corner. "It's Susannah."

Josie froze, pressing the photograph against her chest as if she'd been caught stealing it. She felt her face burn, even though she knew it was ridiculous. This picture had been put out for anyone to see. She wasn't prying into anyone's personal affairs.

She wasn't doing anything to be ashamed of.

But the other woman looked at her with such a cool, quiet disapproval that it was hard to remember that. Awkwardly, Josie pried the picture away from her chest and held it out for Susannah to see.

"Hello," she said. "I was just waiting for Chase to come home. I was just looking at these family pictures he has out here."

No kidding. She sounded like a complete simpleton. And she sounded guilty as hell.

"Hi, Josie. You're looking better. How are you feeling?"

Susannah didn't take the picture, so Josie set it back down on the credenza, bumping into two others.

"Much better," she said, though she was getting tired of giving that same response to everyone. Too bad good manners prevented you from answering with the truth. *My head hurts, I feel like puking and frankly I'm scared to death.*

"I'm glad," Susannah said, though you couldn't tell it by looking at her.

Josie hadn't been clearheaded enough to really look at Susannah last night. She'd just been this shadowy, gentle figure in the background, listening while Josie told her story.

But now Josie could see that this was one of the coolest, most collected women she'd ever met. Susannah Everly was a true beauty, with glossy hair, sparkling green eyes and the athletic, long-limbed body of a dancer.

Her posture and wardrobe said she'd been raised with confidence and class. She wore three-hundred-dollar jeans, a sharp white shirt with a dashing cut and a turned-up collar. Her long legs ended in fawn-colored boots that looked as soft as butter.

She moved gracefully into the room and, though she tried to make it look casual, she scanned the set of photographs, as if checking for missing spots.

"I didn't steal one," Josie heard herself saying. "If that's what you're thinking."

Josie inhaled sharply, shocked that she'd actually spoken the words out loud. That was unbelievably rude.

It didn't seem to faze Susannah, though. She merely smiled, as cool as ever. "Of course you didn't. I just realized I haven't looked at them in a long time myself. Some of these go way back, to when we were kids."

Josie glanced at the photograph of the laughing teens, giddy with youth. "You've known him a long time."

"Since I was born. Our families have lived on these adjoining spreads for generations. He was my best friend long before he was my fiancé."

"How nice." Josie didn't trust herself to say more. She dreaded the thought that she might sound bitter. But it brought home, didn't it, how stupid she'd been to believe Chase Clayton IV would come looking for love in the Not Guilty Café. When people like this wanted a partner, they didn't need to look farther than the ranch next door.

She wondered if Susannah was deliberately trying to make her feel like an outsider. If so, it was overkill. She already felt so *other* she might as well have been from a different planet.

"Susannah, do you mind if we cut through all the polite, surface things we're supposed to say here, and just be completely candid?"

"Of course not." Susannah looked curious, but not offended. Josie wondered what it would take to disturb a woman this cool. "Of course you should say anything you want."

"Thanks." Josie's head had begun to throb. She tried to ignore it.

"It's just that—I can tell there's a lot going on beneath the surface here. I've tried to be honest. I admitted my mistake. But with you, the lawyer, the doctor, even Chase, it's as if we're polite adversaries. There's always that hint of suspicion. Why is that? It seems to me we're all pretty much in the same boat. Victims of the man who impersonated Chase."

The other woman took a deep breath. "You're right, of course. It's not fair. I guess it's because… because we all love him."

Josie frowned. "But what—"

"We're protective of him, I think. That sounds strange, because he's so strong, and really he's the one who always protects all of us." She touched one of the pictures. Josie thought it was the one of the teenagers.

"He's a good person, Josie. One of the best people you'll ever meet."

"I don't doubt that. He's been very nice, nicer than he had to be. But why does he need protecting from me? I'm no threat to him."

· Susannah smiled. "That's probably true. Still. You have to admit it's all very strange. The way you arrived, the story you tell…"

"I know. I am as bewildered as any of you. Probably more so."

"Yes, of course. But Chase is a very prominent man, and that draws a lot of...unwanted attention. It wouldn't be the first time someone tried to fleece him. No one has done it successfully, though—not in a long, long time."

Josie felt her back stiffen. *"Fleece?"*

"I didn't mean that you..." Susannah sighed. "Damn it. I'm not expressing myself very well."

"No, I think I understand you perfectly. Let me recap. Chase Clayton is a rich, important hotshot, and I'm a suspicious nobody from nowhere. And if I plan to sue, rob, slander or otherwise annoy him I'd better be careful, because his equally prominent friends are standing guard."

Susannah seemed about to protest, but Josie's look stopped her.

"All right, fair enough, though I believe you'll discover we're not quite the snobs you think we are." Susannah seemed to square her shoulders. "But there's one more thing I came here to tell you."

"What?"

She put her cool, slim hand on Josie's arm. Her beautiful face was grave.

"If what you say is true, there's a man out there who has done an incredibly cruel thing. A terrible, unforgivable thing. Not just to Chase. *To you.* And if there's any way I can help you find him, Josie, I will."

CHASE DIDN'T SEE his houseguest for a full twenty-four hours. He meant to check on her, but things kept cropping up. One of his most promising stallions stressed a tendon when something spooked him in the turnout paddock. The south stable's new roof sprang a leak during the regular afternoon downpour. Late in the afternoon, Eli Breslin, the new stable boy, broke the mechanical cow, and Chase had to keep Boss Johnson, his best cutting horse trainer, from drop-kicking the kid into the next county.

Thank God for Imogene, who was half drill sergeant, half Mother Teresa. He knew he could trust her to give Josie plenty of TLC, while at the same time keeping an eagle eye on her, just in case there was, after all, a con artist lurking beneath that wounded-baby-bird exterior.

By the time Chase got back to the house, both Josie and Imogene had gone to bed. Frankly, he was too tired to be anything but relieved.

But the next morning, after a quick meeting with Trent, he knocked on the guest room door.

Josie answered quickly, as if she'd been waiting. She wore the same clothes she'd had on yesterday, just a pair of jeans and a brown T-shirt. He wondered if he should buy her something else…or maybe ask Sue to do it.

"Morning," he said. "Did you sleep well? You look like you feel better."

That was only partly true. Her bad eye actually looked even worse, as the raccoon-black bruising began to lighten to a sickly mishmash of purple, yellow and red. But her good eye looked much better.

The blue had a real sparkle, the whites weren't bloodshot, and the circle underneath had begun to disappear.

"Thanks," she said. "Although I do have a mirror in here, you know, so gallantry can only go so far."

He smiled. "The *right* side of you looks tons better, and that's not gallantry. It's the truth." He reached out to free a strand of silky, honey-brown hair from the tape that held down the gauze of her forehead bandage. "The left side will follow. Just give it time."

She nodded, but she tilted her head back slightly. He wondered if he'd made her uncomfortable by touching her, even this casually. It would make his lawyer uncomfortable, no doubt. Stilling always saw everything in terms of how it would sound in court.

Did you ever touch the plaintiff, Mr. Clayton?

"Imogene tells me you were going stir-crazy yesterday, looking for something to do."

"A little. She gave me a few chores, but I still feel pretty useless."

"You shouldn't. Your job is to recuperate."

That apparently was the wrong answer. Her softly arched brows drove together.

"I'm not an invalid, for heaven's sake. I just have a black eye and a couple of stitches." One side of her mouth cocked up reluctantly. "And diabetes. And morning sickness."

"And anemia."

"And a couple of guys running jackhammers in my head." She gave up and grinned. "But other than that I'm fine."

"Good. You'll be glad to hear, then, that I've got a mission for you."

Now her eyes really did sparkle, even the multicolored one. "Yes. Anything!"

"Trent rounded up some pictures for me. I thought we could look at them and see if you recognize anybody." The phone on his belt began to beep. "Sorry," he said, and answered it.

It was Boss Johnson. Another crisis. The red roan they recently bought, a horse

Johnson had high hopes for, was acting up.
Johnson thought the stallion might have a
phobia about bright colors.

Great. Just what he needed. Pay all
outdoors for a horse who balked every
time a cardinal flew by.

"I'll be there in five." Chase clicked off
the phone with a sigh. The truth was, he
didn't have time to play Sherlock Holmes
with this woman. He really should hire a
private detective to track down the elusive
Mr. Flim and send little Josie Whitford
home to Riverfork.

"Is everything all right?" She bit her
lower lip, which had the effect of making
Chase stare at her mouth. It was, he
noticed, pretty fantastic. Wide and full,
with a built-in pucker that had all kinds of
X-rated undertones.

For the first time, he understood why
Flim had chosen this particular woman to
seduce. That was a mighty fine mouth.

A shiver passed through him, settling
in his loins.

Somehow he pulled the thoughts up

short and turned off the heat. What the hell was he doing, letting himself ride into murky territory like that?

Oh, yeah, he sure as hell needed to get her back to Riverfork.

But then he made the mistake of raising his gaze and looking straight into her blue eyes.

Damn it, those eyes belonged on someone else. On one of those Hallmark card kids, maybe, the waifs who crouched in corners, their faces too small to hold their round, sad, innocent eyes.

It was the eyes, in the end, that made the decision for him.

"Yeah, everything's okay. I need to go check out one of the new horses, though." He holstered his phone. "We could do this a little later…or…"

She cocked her head. "Or?"

Dumb, Clayton. Really dumb.

But he said it anyway.

"Or you could come along with me."

CHAPTER SEVEN

JOHNSON BROUGHT the roan into the outdoor round pen to demonstrate the problem. The side boards would cut down on distractions.

It took only about two minutes for Chase to see that the trainer was right.

Damn it. The horse still looked gorgeous. Healthy. Athletic. Good conformation. He had a light mouth—Johnson hardly had to touch the reins. Chase already knew that the stallion had been trained for cutting by somebody who knew his stuff. He used his hindquarters well, stopped on a dime with his hocks buried in the sand, and kept his head low, even on his backups and spins.

Even better, he liked it. That was the magic. Any good trainer could teach a horse to cut cattle, but only God could make him like it.

Then came the heartbreaker. At a prearranged signal, Eli Breslin, the nineteen-year-old ranch hand who had broken the mechanical cow yesterday, entered the pen, wearing a bright red shirt. Instantly the confident, cooperative roan began to balk. He backed up, shook his head from side to side and threatened to rear.

It was all Johnson could do to hold him. The same stallion who had responded to the lightest touch of the reins against his neck now ignored the thrust of a cold bit, hard in his mouth, and the pressure of Johnson's powerful legs.

"Enough." Chase made a sawing motion in the air, telling Johnson to give it up. Johnson jerked a thumb to dismiss Eli, and the boy exited quickly, looking relieved.

Johnson dismounted. Immediately the horse subsided, though his ears lay flat against his head, and his nostrils were flared. This was not a happy animal.

Chase wasn't a happy rancher, either. He conferred with Johnson another minute, and then he exited the pen, trying to shake off his frustration before he got to the viewing stands, where he'd left Josie with the photos.

Instead, she was standing two feet away, in a shaft of sunlight on the other side of the door.

"I hope you don't mind—I climbed up so I could watch," she said. "I'm sorry, Chase. That didn't go well, did it?"

"No." He shook his head. "Damn shame, too. That could have been a champion. He has it all."

"Can it be fixed? Can you train him not to be so afraid?"

"Maybe. Maybe not. Depends on the horse, and how he got the phobia in the first place. It's a lot of work, no matter how you look at it."

"But you'll try?"

He shrugged, casting one last glance into the pen, where Johnson was soothing the still-agitated roan. "I don't know. I'm not sure it's cost-effective."

Josie frowned. "You mean you'd just give up on him? A horse that could have been a champion? Just because he's had some kind of trauma in his past?"

"Probably. It's disappointing, but that's how it goes sometimes. Not every horse lives up to its potential. We'll find another one."

She tilted her head. "Is that how it is on a ranch? No room for mistakes? You're either perfect, or you're off to the glue factory?"

He squinted at her, trying to block enough of the sun to get a look at her face. He couldn't read her expression, but all five foot three of her was rigid with disapproval. He wondered whether they were still talking about the roan.

"I'm a rancher, Josie. Not the horse whisperer. But if it makes you feel any better we don't send our animals to the glue factory. We'll find someone who wants a good horse at a good price, someone who has the time to correct it."

She remained stiff for another moment, and then all the starch just blew out of her.

"I'm sorry," she said, shaking her head. "I don't know what got into me. It's just that he was such a sweet horse, and it seems so unfair. It's not his fault if something terrible happened to him—"

She put her hands over her face. "God, listen to me! I've been here two days and I'm already telling you how to run your business. Forget I said anything, please. It's none of my business." She tried to smile. "Shall we talk about the pictures?"

"Sure." He put his hand behind her shoulder and nudged her slightly toward the viewing stands, where she'd left the packet of photographs. They walked slowly together across the grass, the sunlight in their eyes. It was going to be a hot one. It was almost as if spring had come and gone in the span of about a week.

"Did you get a chance to look at them all? Did anyone seem familiar?"

"I'm not sure," she said. "Most of them, no. They may have a superficial resemblance, but they're not him."

When they reached the stand, they sat on the first bleacher, straddling it like a pommel, with the manila envelope between them.

He opened it and drew out the dozen or so photographs Trent had found. On such short notice, some of them were far from ideal. They were clearly things he'd borrowed from the Double C scrapbook, or printouts of photos that turned up on the Internet. One was a grainy, black-and-white crowd scene from the local newspaper.

Very few of them had the full-face clarity of a mug shot. But, for now, they'd have to do.

As he shuffled through them, Chase was glad to see that Trent had followed directions to the letter. He'd included a few fillers, the way the police would do when creating a lineup of robbery suspects. A few extra pictures, just random people who matched Flim's general description.

It wasn't that Chase didn't trust Josie, it was just that…

Okay. So he didn't trust her. Not one hundred percent, anyhow. He didn't care how waifish or sexy or whatever she was. There was still one percent of him that said he'd be a sucker to simply shove a picture of his cousin, Alexander, under her nose and say, "Is this the guy?"

He handed them to her in a pile, without speaking. "Tell me what you think."

She flipped through the stack quickly. "No. No." She stared at one of the photos, tilting it for better light. "He's very like this." She handed the photograph to Chase. "It's not him, but it's close."

He looked at it without comment. It was one of the filler shots, probably some guy from copyright-free clip art on Trent's computer. Good-looking guy, though. Not unlike Alexander, really.

He put it down. "Okay. We'll remember that. Go on."

She was methodical, taking each one seriously, but always ending up with a *no*. He watched, keeping his face completely immobile.

So…it wasn't Marx, the guy who'd been ticked about the Hillman land sale. Too bad. Marx was married, and smart enough to realize he'd have to pay fair child support, if only to avoid the scandal.

And it wasn't Charming Billy, the wrangler with the roving hands, either. Well, that was a good thing. Chase had heard that Billy had been fired from every spread in East Texas. He'd be nothing but a liability. Josie could end up with two babies on her hands, one of them six feet tall.

Finally she had the stack narrowed down to one last photograph.

"I don't really think this is Flim," she said, clearly discouraged. Her shoulders sagged, and he wondered if she was getting tired. "It could be, I guess. The profile is similar, and…I don't know…something about the posture. But it's not a very good picture, and it must be from a long time ago. Chase—I mean Flim—is at least ten years older than this man."

He took the picture. She was right—it was an old one. It had been taken about ten years ago, at a Christmas party at the Double C.

"I just don't now." She bit her lower lip again. "If I could see him from the front, full-face…"

The Flim look-alike wasn't even the

focal point of the photograph. He was just standing in the background, drinking whiskey and flirting with an extremely elegant brunette woman.

With Lila Clayton, to be exact. Chase's first wife. It was, in fact, the last Clayton party this guy had ever been invited to. He'd gotten drunk and made a scene with Lila. And then, the next year, he'd gone to Vegas and stuck Chase's stolen ATM card into the slot machine.

Chase leaned back on his elbows, letting the photograph drop on the wooden seat between his knees.

Damn it. Of course, it was the biggest sleazeball in the batch.

It was Cousin Alexander.

As THE WAITER REFILLED her water glass, Susannah fidgeted with the Belgian lace that draped her upper arm. The stuff was pretty to look at, but so darned distracting. And it tickled, too.

She hadn't worn so many girlie dresses in a row since she was old enough to choose her own clothes. She'd forgotten how much she hated them.

But though her own taste ran more to no-fuss, tailored clothes, she knew that most men preferred things lacy and sweet. Lacy and slutty would be even better, but she wasn't willing to go that far, not even to land Ken Longstreet's restaurant chain as an outlet for her peaches.

"Your wife and I have worked together for years, raising money for the Burn Center." She smiled. "I'll bet you've even eaten my peach cobbler at one of the fund-raisers."

"Maybe. Can't say I remember," Ken responded, his mouth still half-full of rib eye and mashed potatoes. "I've eaten Everly peaches, of course. My sister likes 'em in her pie. She's a spinster from over in Sundown—nothing much going on way out there, so she's got plenty of time to cook."

Susannah tried to keep smiling. But good grief. She didn't even know people used the world *spinster* anymore. She wished she had accepted Jim Stilling's offer to come along as a buffer. Jim could blow clouds of good-ole-boy smoke when he needed to. She could have thrown in a dimple and a smile now and then, and a few awed murmurs, like "You don't say!" or "Why, that's amazing."

And the deal would have been signed, sealed and delivered by dessert.

"So you really run that big orchard all by yourself?" He waved his fork at her, apparently unaware that a ribbon of rib eye fat still clung to the tines. "That ain't right. A pretty little thing like you?"

Susannah gritted her teeth so hard she nearly cracked a filling. She hated millionaire Yale MBAs who talked pseudo-hillbilly, thinking it would cloak their obnoxious chauvinism. Her foot twitched. If she kicked him under the table with one of these miserably uncomfortable spiky heels, could she make him believe it was an accident?

Brilliant, Sue. She was actually considering kicking the one guy in Texas who might be able to save her ranch.

She tucked her foot behind her ankle

and squeezed it in place. Maybe her grandfather was right—she wasn't sweet enough to be a good woman, and she wasn't tough enough to be a good man.

"It's not easy, Ken," she said, pouring a little syrup over the words. "But you know I'm getting married soon, and Chase will be able to help me make the big decisions."

Damn if the creep didn't actually look relieved. "That's true. There's a certain amount of security there. I know Chase, of course. He's a hell of a businessman."

"Yes." She took a sip of water and counted to three. Then she smiled deeply enough to bring out the dimple. "So you see, if you decide to contract with Everly Orchards, you can be absolutely sure that—"

Her cell phone trilled.

Damn it. Her instincts told her that Ken didn't like interruptions.

"Oh, I'm so sorry," she said. She reached her hand into her drawstring purse, pulled out the little silver rectangle, and checked the caller ID.

It was Nicole. Susannah felt a pulse beat

at the edge of her jaw. Nikki knew about this dinner, and she knew how important it was. Susannah thumbed the ignore button and put the phone in her lap.

"Now." Leaning her elbows on the tablecloth, she laced her fingers and rested her chin on them. "Where were we?"

"The contract," he said, pushing aside the small vase of orchids, so that he could lean in a little closer. "You were reminding me that, in a few months, Chase Clayton will be—"

The phone rang again.

She looked down. Nicole again.

"Maybe you'd better take that." Ken's fleshy face had turned a shade or two redder, and his voice sounded much more arrogant Yale, less backwoods bumpkin. "Doesn't sound as if they plan to take no for an answer."

She smiled apologetically. "Yes, I'm sorry. It's my little sister. I'll just be a minute."

She clicked the answer button.

"Nikki," she said, putting an edge in the greeting. "Is everything all right?"

"No." Nicole sounded angry. "I need you to come get me."

"Where are you?"

"I'm at Greta's party."

Damn it. They'd been over and over this earlier today, and Susannah had refused to budge. No parties on weeknights. But Nicole was getting more and more brazen, and the argument had turned ugly.

For the first time, Susannah had said the B word.

Boarding school.

She had hoped the threat worked. But apparently she'd been kidding herself. It had probably just goaded Nikki into doing something even more rash. God only knew how she'd gotten to the party.

"You're at Greta's party. That's interesting." She had to keep her tone pleasant, but she squeezed in the special hint of lemon that Nicole would recognize. And she'd know it meant trouble.

"Yeah, I bet." Nicole's voice was hostile, but it also sounded kind of stuffy, as if she'd been crying. "Look, Sue, you really need to come get me. Eli was supposed to be here, but he didn't show up."

So that explained the tears. Eli had stood her up. Well, too darn bad. Nikki had insisted on going to the blasted party, in spite of everything Susannah had said. Now she'd just have to live with that decision.

"I'm afraid that's not possible," Susannah said. "I'm tied up right now."

"Come on, Sue. I want to go home. You're not going to be a bitch about this, are you?"

"Yes," she responded sweetly. "I'm afraid I am."

There was a silence.

"Fine. Be that way." A rough sniffing sound. "God, I hate you sometimes."

And then the phone went dead.

She lowered it slowly to her lap again and looked over at Ken Longstreet. He had a feathery dollop of mashed potato caught in the left edge of his mustache, and a dime-sized gravy stain on his expensive white shirt. Apparently his Yale career hadn't included a class in table manners.

"Done?" He glanced at his Rolex. "Can we get back to business?"

"Yes," Susannah said awkwardly. But then she shook her head. What if it wasn't just Eli's absence that had spoiled the party for Nik? What if there were really something wrong?

"No. I'm sorry. I need to—just one more thing…"

Ignoring Ken's surprised scowl, she picked up the phone and, typing as fast as she could, began putting together a text message to Chase.

Nik stuck at Greta Sugarton party, any chance you're free to…

Oh, well, she thought as she hit Send.

She had probably lost Ken Longstreet's business now, judging from the look on his face. And she'd probably lose all credibility with Nikki, too.

Maybe it really was a good thing she

would marry Chase soon. Maybe this was just one more piece of proof, as if she'd needed it, that her grandfather had been right.

She really wasn't tough enough to make it on her own.

CHAPTER EIGHT

CHASE HAD BEEN IN AUSTIN with Josie that afternoon, talking to a sketch artist, who tried to make a visual out of Josie's description of Flim. Unfortunately, it didn't look like anyone he recognized, although it bore a superficial resemblance to Alexander.

Josie felt dissatisfied. The sketch was close, but not really right. Maybe she wasn't describing him right. But both she and the artist had done the best they could. Chase decided to start by tracking down Alexander. At the moment it was their only real clue.

They were on their way home when he got Susannah's text message. He could read between the lines. Sue was a nervous wreck, not knowing what Nikki might do. He asked Josie if she minded making a detour by Greta Sugarton's house.

What a trouper she was. Though he could tell she was tired, she wouldn't hear of letting him take her all the way back to the ranch. Nikki should come first.

Unfortunately, Nikki had already left the party. Chase checked everyone out—and opened a big can of buzz-kill on that brainless Greta and her friends, most of whom were barfing up her daddy's fifty-dollar whiskey on his fifty-thousand-dollar lawn.

Then he decided to check the main road back to Everly. He had a feeling Nik was too smart to have hitched a ride home with any of these sot-faced losers.

His headlights picked her out, trudging along on the easement, about two miles from the party, maybe seven miles from Everly. He flipped his brights twice to get her attention, then slowed to a crawl beside her and rolled down his window.

"Umm…did you see my thumb out, buster?" Her voice was acid, and she didn't even turn around to look at him. "I didn't think so. Because I'm not looking for a ride."

"Well, good, because I'm not looking to pick up any bad-tempered little brats, either."

She turned around. "Chase!" Her smile was pure relief. "Boy, am I glad to see you."

Then she noticed Josie in the passenger seat. She gave Chase a weird look.

He smiled. "Nicole Everly, this is Josie Whitford, a friend of mine from Riverfork."

Josie smiled, and Nikki nodded stiffly. "Hi."

Then apparently she decided to pretend Josie wasn't there. Without preamble, she pulled open the truck's back door and climbed in. She reached down and began peeling off her sandals. "Thank God you showed up. My feet are killing me in these stupid shoes."

Chase had already noticed the strappy sandals with the three-inch heels. Susannah would have a stroke if she saw how Nikki was dressed.

"Yes, ma'am," he said with a smile. "Those are just about the stupidest shoes I ever saw. Why the devil are you wearing them? Have you got your brain out on loan to somebody?"

He heard them drop on the floor. "They're sexy. Eli likes them." She scowled at him in the rearview mirror, drawing her brows down over her heavily made-up eyes. "Hey, that's right. I'm not speaking to you. It's all your fault that Eli couldn't come to the party tonight. You're a slave driver. Doesn't he ever get any time off?"

Chase watched the road, picking his next sentence carefully. He thought Eli was a pretty good kid—in spite of the mechanical cow fiasco—but he knew that Sue felt their three-year age difference was a big problem. Maybe he should remind her that she'd fallen in love with Trent when she was even younger than Nikki.

Then again, the love affair with Trent hadn't gone that well, so maybe it wasn't the best comparison in the world. Still. If Sue didn't back off, the kids were probably going to end up stealing a couple of his horses and eloping to Reno.

"Eli gets time off if he gets his work

done. That's how it is in the grown-up world, Nik. He can't be out boozing and puking all night, because he's got to punch a time clock in the morning."

She screwed up her plum-colored lips. "I guess that means you went by Greta's party."

"Was that a party? I thought I'd stumbled into the monkey house at the zoo."

"I know." She heaved a big sigh. "Wasn't it gross? There's going to be trouble there tonight, I just know it. That's why I wanted to get the heck out of there. Some of those boys are…" She pulled at her big, dangly earring. "You don't know where I can get some mace, do you?"

He gave her a hard look in the mirror. "Did somebody get out of line with you?"

"Well, Elton Barnes is a jackass even when he's sober, which he most definitely wasn't, so I had to kick him in the…"

She glanced toward Josie. Chase looked over at her, too, and realized that she was smiling.

"In the family jewels," Nikki finished.
"Ouch."

She grinned. "Yeah, that's what he said. Only louder. So you don't have to worry. I can take care of myself. It's just that mace would be so much easier. I almost broke my shoe."

He chuckled. "And that would have been a terrible shame." He glanced in the mirror again and nodded. "Okay. I'll look into some pepper spray, if you want it. But don't tell Sue."

"Like she'd care. The only thing that she even thinks about anymore is the ranch. And her stupid volunteer work at the Burn Center. Hey, I know, maybe she'd notice me if I set myself on fire."

He drove in silence for a couple of minutes, trying to decide whether it would be better to stay out of it. Sue and Nikki were obviously having a tough time these days.

Inevitable, he supposed. After the disaster with Trent and Paul, Sue had changed. She'd always been a levelheaded gal, a calming influence on the three hard-headed boys. But after that night...well, it was as though her internal heater just up and broke. You couldn't quite accuse her of being cold, but her spigots seemed to run nothing but cool. No whimsy, no foolishness, no fun. No mistakes of her own, and no tolerance for other people's, either.

Not exactly the perfect guardian for an eccentric little rascal like Nik.

"Susannah told me why you guys are really getting married," Nikki said. She had turned her head toward the window.

He glanced at Josie one more time. He hadn't discussed any of this with her yet. Why would he? There was no earthly reason she needed to know the details of his engagement to Susannah, and yet, now that Nikki had brought it up, he felt slightly uncomfortable, as if he'd been caught hiding something.

"Oh, really?" He kept his voice noncommittal, hoping against hope that Nikki would, for the first time in her life, show some restraint.

No such luck.

"Yeah," Nikki said. "Not that I was exactly

surprised. I knew there had to be a catch. No man in his right mind would actually be in love with a cold fish like Susannah."

He sensed Josie's surprise, as she moved slightly, her profile tilting toward him, just an inch or so. But she didn't say anything, obviously realizing that this might be a sensitive topic.

In spite of his reluctance to discuss it all in front of her, Chase couldn't let a comment like that go. He thought of Trent, and Paul, and countless other men whose hearts Sue had broken through the years.

"Hey, squirt. Easy on your sister there. You couldn't be more wrong. I only decided to be her friend because the line to fall in love with her was way too long."

Nikki shrugged. "Still, it seems really weird that you'd get married like a business deal. Don't you want a real wedding, with flowers and music and people crying and everything?"

He shifted his hand on the steering wheel. Well, it was all going to come out now, wasn't it? "God, no. I already had one of those, remember? And that was one too many."

"Oh, yeah." Nikki swiveled to face Josie. "Did you know Chase was married before? Her name was Lila."

Chase groaned inwardly. Josie was certainly getting an earful tonight. He wondered whether Nikki was doing this deliberately. Did she think Josie was somehow a threat to Susannah? Given how lukewarm Nikki seemed to be about the engagement, that didn't seem likely.

This was why he spent most of his time with horses. Women ran too deep for him. Even sixteen-year-old women.

"I've seen Lila's picture," Nikki added. "She was pretty. But I don't really remember her."

"Of course not. You were much too young. Hell, *I* was much too young."

Finally, Josie spoke up. "How old were you?"

"Nineteen. Lila was twenty-five. My mom had just died, and I think I was probably looking for a mother substitute."

Nikki made a hacking sound. "Gross!"

"I'm just kidding. Actually, she was gorgeous, and sweet as one of your Everly peaches. At least until we tied the knot. Then she started complaining about everything, from the way I combed my hair to the color of the sky on Tuesday. She didn't stop until we signed the divorce papers."

"And she took all your money, right? That's what Susannah says. She says it cost your dad a fortune to get rid of Lila, but it was worth it."

Josie chuckled. It was a surprisingly attractive sound. He hadn't heard her laugh much since she'd arrived.

"It was worth it," he agreed, smiling. It had been extremely painful at the time, but a whole decade had passed, and he could see how ridiculous he'd been. "I pretty much just went up to her and said, 'Listen here, woman, how much money will it take to make you quit your bitching and go away?'"

Nikki giggled, still young enough to think it was funny to hear him say "bitching." But she sobered quickly. She acted tough, but Chase knew she had a sensitive side, just like her sister. The only difference was that, while Susannah hid hers under all that icy control, Nikki used a smoke screen of badass attitude.

"That must have really sucked," she said. "So why are you going to do it all over again?"

"Do what again?"

"Marry someone who just wants your money."

He pulled into the driveway of the Everly Ranch. Sue's car was here, and he could picture her pacing the front hall, waiting for his call. He wished he could get her alone, and warn her not to be too rough on Nikki. The kid hadn't done everything wrong tonight. She'd been smart to get away from that party, and she'd been smart to refuse rides from strangers.

And she needed to know that Susannah loved her, even when she screwed up.

He swerved the car to the side of the drive, a few yards out from the house, then turned to face Nikki. He needed to set her straight about something. He didn't want her judging her sister so harshly—especially not in front of Josie.

"Susannah isn't marrying me for my money," he said. "I can't tell you how many times I've offered to help her out, to just give her whatever she needs to get the ranch back on an even keel. But she won't take it. What she needs is freedom, the power to run this ranch the way it should be run. Because of the will, she'll never have that unless she gets married."

He wasn't really getting through to her, he could tell. Her features looked very young, and lost under all that makeup. Her eyes looked tired, damaged by the layers of color—poignantly reminiscent of Josie's real bruises.

Susannah had spotted them. She opened the front door and came out onto the porch. She looked beautiful. She wore something feminine that had lace at the neck and arms.

"Chase? Is Nikki with you?" Susannah descended the steps and hurried toward the truck.

"Well, speak of the devil." Nikki opened her door. Then she turned and looked at him, her colorful face bizarre in the sudden flare of the dome light. "I still think you're both nuts. Nobody should marry for anything but love."

Chase got out, too, and somehow reached Susannah before Nikki did.

"Don't bring out the big guns," he said. "She's had a tough night."

Susannah looked at him. Then she glanced toward the car, where Josie sat quietly waiting. He started to explain why Josie was there, but he stopped himself. Trying to justify one woman to another was like taking the first step into quicksand.

Especially when you had this many women in your life.

"Okay," Susannah said under her breath. "It won't be easy, but I'll try not to kill her."

"Good girl," he said. He gave her a quick kiss on the cheek. "I'll check in tomorrow if I get a chance."

She nodded. Then he got back to the car and started the engine.

Josie spoke quietly into the darkness. "Everything okay?"

"I hope so. I have a feeling it's going to be ugly, though." He made a three-point turn and headed out the front gates, which gleamed white in the moonlight. "Poor dumb kid."

They drove in silence a minute or two. When they hit the main road again, Josie put her hand out and touched his forearm.

"Just for the record," she said, "I don't think what you're doing for Susannah is nuts. I think it's very generous, and... very gallant."

He tightened his hand on the wheel, intensely aware of her, of how she smelled, like soap and shampoo and something... something warm and female.

He sensed the silkiness of the skin on the pads of her fingers. He felt each one individually, and he imagined how they'd feel if they roamed to other places of his body.

He thought about how close she'd be to him, all night, right there in his guest room. It would be so easy to open that door, and...

A crazy heat began to stir at the tops of his thighs.

Oh, hell, no. Not again.

He couldn't help responding to her. It was pure physical instinct. Mindless reflex. His body was primed, because they'd been talking about love, and marriage and sex.

No, they hadn't been talking about sex. But he realized that he'd been *thinking* about sex. About how Nikki just might have zeroed in on a truth. A year of a "business deal" marriage to his best friend meant a year without a woman in his bed.

A week ago, that hadn't sccmcd like a problem. He wasn't a beast. He could control himself for that long.

But now...now he wasn't so sure.

Josie squeezed his arm gently. It wasn't a come-on. It was just a friendly sign of support. So why did it send this sizzle straight to the hot spot between his legs?

Damn it. This didn't mean anything.

It *couldn't* mean anything.

He was engaged to someone else.

She was pregnant with another man's child.

He eased his arm away, pretending he needed to fiddle with the mirror.

Gallant? She actually thought he was gallant?

"Remember, we've got an appointment with the obstetrician in the morning," he said. "So when we get home, you'd better go right to sleep."

And, if you know what's good for you, lock the goddamn door.

That's how *gallant* he was.

"WE DATE THE PREGNANCY from the onset of the last menstrual cycle," Dr. Dunne said, spreading out her paperwork on his big mahogany desk. There were snapshots of newborns everywhere. He must have delivered every baby in East Texas.

"But given that you aren't always regular, Josie, I'd rather use information from the scan we did today. Which means your due date should be mid-September. Let's say the fifteenth."

Josie nodded numbly. *September fifteenth...* For a minute she felt herself wanting to say *no, that's too soon, we'll have to make it later.*

But the man wasn't asking her permission. The baby was coming, sometime in September, whether she was ready or not.

She wasn't.

The fifteenth of September.

It would be here before she knew it. One long, hot summer, that was all the time she had to get ready. The months would pass in a blur, and then, in a blinding, terrifying miracle, she would hold her own baby in her arms.

A baby she suddenly realized she wanted very much.

And yet she had nothing to give it. Nothing. Not a home, not a dollar, not even a daddy.

Nothing but love.

But oh, she had a lot of that. She'd waited her whole life for someone who would want all this love she had to give. Her father had died when Josie was only six months old. Her mother had remarried when Josie was four, to a man who demanded all his new wife's attention. Her stepfather hadn't wanted children in the first place, so obviously there had been no sisters and brothers.

"Hey," Chase said softly. He touched her elbow. "Are you okay?"

She nodded. For a split second, she'd forgotten he was here.

"Yes. Yes, of course. Fine."

When the doctor had finished examining her, Chase had joined them for the conference. At first, Josie hadn't been sure she'd be comfortable with that. But given that he had found this obstetrician, made the appointment and paid for it, she hadn't felt she should say no when he asked if she wanted company.

As it turned out, she was very glad to have him at her side. This obstetrician wasn't like the general practitioner she'd seen at the clinic. The difference was more than surface, although the office suite, with its glossy walls, gorgeous flowers and soothing Mozart floating out through invisible speakers, was worlds apart from the noisy, bare-bones clinic back in Riverfork.

The real difference, though, was the attention Dr. Dunne lavished on her. He had checked every single inch of her body, asked about every detail of her past. Now he was inundating her with so much information she knew she'd never remember it all.

"You said everything looked good, right?" Chase leaned forward to pick up one of the brochures the doctor had set out for her. "Both Josie and the baby?"

"Everything looked great," Dr. Dunne assured him. "Strong heartbeat, fetal size right on track, and a remarkably healthy mother, all things considered."

He turned to Josie. "Dr. Marchant is already addressing the anemia, which is fairly mild. But the great news is that you've handled your blood sugars remarkably well, Josie, and that's going to pay benefits in this pregnancy."

She nodded. "Good," she said politely, still numb. "That's great."

"You probably don't know exactly how good. Your A1c levels are fantastic, which means that for the past three months the baby has had the best possible environment to grow healthy organs. Most of the risks associated with diabetic pregnancies come from letting the blood sugar levels get out of control during this early period."

"I've always been very careful," she said. "I didn't plan to get pregnant, but my job is very demanding. I can't afford to be sick, or even foggy-minded."

She didn't mention that her habit of strict monitoring, careful eating and rigorous exercise had been set in her very earliest years. Her stepfather had found his adopted daughter's diabetes a great inconvenience. He resented every minute her mother spent caring for her, and every dollar spent on doctors. He wouldn't have tolerated any self-indulgent candy binges, or skipping a day at the jogging track.

How ironic that, in the end, she should be grateful to him for what she'd always seen as his heartlessness. She should send him a thank-you card. Or maybe a box of sugar-free chocolates.

"As to the baby's sex—"

She shook her head. "I don't want to know."

Chase looked at her, a question in his eyes. "It might help with the planning, and—"

She shook her head again. "Please. If you know, don't tell me."

The doctor smiled. "Don't worry. I couldn't make that call yet anyhow. It's a bit early. Maybe at twenty weeks, sometimes as early as sixteen, we can try again. Think it over, and we can talk about it later."

Later? She glanced at Chase, wondering what he had told the doctor about how long she'd be here. But he was looking at the brochure, and she couldn't catch his gaze.

"I'm only staying in town for a few days," she said, deciding on honesty. "I live in Riverfork, and I'll be—"

Chase looked up. "We don't really know exactly how long you'll stay, do we? It might be longer." He turned to Dr. Dunne. "Josie has some business to do here, and she's staying at the ranch. It's a bit open-ended at the moment."

The doctor didn't seem disturbed by the news. He didn't seem to feel that the intricacies of Josie's relationship to Chase were his business. Unless Chase was the father, of course. Dr. Dunne had asked that first, when they were alone. When she said no, he accepted her word for it. He'd simply told her that he would need as much information as possible about the father. Blood type, age, family medical history…

Josie had been mortified. She'd almost blurted out the whole sad story. In the end she simply said that she didn't have those answers right now, but would provide them as soon as she could.

What else could she say? Luckily, Dr. Dunne took it all in stride. Perhaps hers wasn't the first complicated, painful story to walk into his office.

"I can always recommend a good man in Riverfork. Just give me a little notice, and I'll ask around." He spread his hands, palms down, on the desk. "I know I've thrown a lot of information at you. Take some time to absorb it all, and come see me again in two or three days. I want you to get that insulin pump, and let's see how it does."

Josie looked over at Chase again. They'd argued about this all the way over here. She couldn't afford the insulin pump, and that was that. There were lots of benefits to working at the Not Guilty Café— flexible hours, good tips, proximity to her apartment—but health insurance wasn't one of them. She'd always bought private insurance, but she had to keep deductibles sky-high in return for decent premiums.

Chase refused to meet her eyes. He held out his hand to the doctor, said their thanks and their goodbyes, then whisked her out to the car. Apparently he'd taken care of the bill while she was being examined. Or perhaps people like Chase Clayton didn't have to pay cash on the spot like the rest of the world.

She waited until they got to the street to launch her protests.

"Chase, I can't let you do this," she said

for the tenth time. "Weren't you listening to Dr. Dunne? I keep my blood sugar under excellent control the old-fashioned way, one shot at a time. The insulin pump is a luxury, not a necessity."

Chase opened the passenger door of his truck and stepped back to let her in. "Weren't *you* listening? He said that in the second and third trimesters the placenta can release hormones that make you more insulin resistant. Keeping the levels right is going to be much trickier now. The pump will help with that."

Boy, he really had paid attention. She'd forgotten that part, if she'd even heard it in the first place. The truth was, the whole visit had a surreal quality to her. She still couldn't quite believe she was pregnant.

She climbed into the truck, settled herself against the cool leather seats, and waited for him to join her. Then, as he put the key into the ignition, she reached out and stopped him from starting the engine.

"Chase, listen to me."

He let go of the keys. "I'll listen if you'll

make sense. You need the pump, and that's a fact. You're not scared of it, are you? I know it sounds strange, having the needle in you all the time, but—"

She smiled. "I've had thousands of insulin injections over the past twenty years. I'm not afraid. It's just not something I can let you do. I can't take money from you. It's a very generous offer, but… this just isn't your problem."

He tilted his head, his blue eyes catching the afternoon sunlight. He had kind eyes, she thought. Even when he was annoyed, which he clearly was right now.

"Not my problem?" He frowned. "I thought we were working together here. I thought we'd agreed that this was a problem we shared."

"Finding Flim is the problem we share. Not the pregnancy. And certainly not my diabetes." She shook her head. "I know you probably think, because of the crazy way I showed up at your ranch, that I'm some kind of kook who can't be trusted to take care of anything. But you heard the doctor. I *do* take care of my blood sugar. And I *will* take care of my baby."

For a long minute, he was silent. The only sound was the drumming of his fingers against the steering wheel. She wondered if she'd made him mad. She hoped not. She wasn't a complete ingrate—she did appreciate how much he'd done for her.

But he already had too many people counting on him, trying to slip their hands in his pockets. After what she'd heard about Susannah Everly last night…

And, besides, there had to be a limit. She had to hold on to *some* self-respect.

Finally he turned to her. He looked frustrated, but not angry. She let go of a breath she had unconsciously been holding. She realized she'd been waiting to see whether he was at all like her stepfather—a hot-tempered control-freak, set off by the least show of defiance.

"I know I'm under no obligation to help," he said simply. "But you haven't considered the possibility that I *want* to.

Look, it's not that much money, and I have it to spare. That part means nothing to me. There are no strings attached, Josie. I'd just like to make things a little easier. Is that so bad?"

The humility in his voice, the down-to-earth honesty, caught her off guard. She felt herself choking up again, and tried to will her hormones into submission.

"It's not bad. It's very generous. But if I do that…" She squeezed her hands in her lap. "I can't just give up every shred of pride I have left."

He touched her shoulder softly. "I think you can," he said. "I saw your face in there. For this baby, I think you can do whatever you have to do."

CHAPTER NINE

THE OLDE MISSION WOODS development, where Chase's cousin, Alexander, now worked as a salesman, had no olde mission, no woods and not much development, either.

Chase slid his truck into one of the parking spaces and surveyed the area irritably. Wouldn't you just know Alexander would end up working at a place like this? Selling smoke and mirrors to the unsuspecting masses.

For the moment, Olde Mission Woods was just a barren stretch of land a few miles northwest of San Antonio. The owners had put up a two-story concrete-block box, slapped some adobe siding on it, added arched windows, a bell tower and a turquoise sign that said Sales Center.

Instant Olde Mission.

That and three windswept models of medium-sized ranch homes were the only buildings in sight, although the brochure boasted an architectural rendering of a shady green neighborhood bustling with mommies and kids on bicycles and expensive SUVs in the driveways.

"What a joke," he said. "*Olde?* Maybe about two weeks. *Mission?* Only if your mission is making money. *Woods?*"

He gestured toward the dozen or so spindly oaks propped up by orange guy wire. In about fifty years, they might provide the kind of shadc pictured in the brochure, but for now they looked like toothpicks with curly green plastic heads.

Josie smiled. "It's not so bad. It'll look better when it matures. The houses seem reasonably priced and kind of cute. Lots of people would think that owning a home here—or anywhere—was a little slice of heaven."

Her tone wasn't critical, and yet he felt like a jerk. Or worse, a snob. She was right, of course—this was a dream come true for a lot of people. The parking lot was overflowing. Potential buyers swarmed in and out of the model homes, smiling eagerly at the salesmen.

"Okay. Maybe I'm just being nasty because I don't much care for Alexander." And he definitely didn't like the idea that his slick cousin might be the father of Josie's baby. "So. Are you ready?"

"Yeah. I guess so."

She didn't sound sure. She fidgeted with her yellow blouse, which was a little too big. He knew she'd bought it because it was on sale, not because she particularly liked it. He'd watched her at the store, checking the price tag over and over, as if trying to convince herself that it was the sensible decision.

She hadn't been willing to let him buy her anything, of course. Not even a fresh pair of socks. He'd never met a woman more prickly about her independence.

Even the prospect of facing Flim here today hadn't budged her.

Chase hadn't pushed. Two days ago, he had won the victory of the insulin pump, and for now that was enough. Besides, he was secretly glad that she didn't obsess about getting new clothes. He wanted to believe it meant she was over Flim, that she wasn't dreaming of rekindling the affair, that looking pretty for her lost lover no longer mattered.

But he wasn't sure. Without spending any money, she'd still taken special pains with her appearance. Marchant had removed her stitches yesterday, and she'd seemed delighted to graduate to an inconspicuous tan bandage. This morning, she'd carefully applied powder to the fading bruises around her eye, and brought out a lipstick and blush he hadn't even realized she owned.

She looked terrific, actually—and he gave himself some of the credit for that. This little respite, in which she'd eaten well, rested well, taken her iron pills, and been tended by some of the best medical men in the business, had worked miracles. He wouldn't have recognized her as the haggard woman who crashed into his front yard ten days ago.

"You don't have to go in if you don't want to." He fought the urge to touch her cheek and try to coax a smile onto those serious lips. "I can take a picture with my cell, and we can see if you recognize him."

"No. I want to do it. That's why we're here." She adjusted her blouse one more time and squared her shoulders. "I'm not going to chicken out now."

Actually, it wasn't the *whole* reason they were here, though she didn't know that. He could have hired an investigator to get a current, full-face shot of Alexander and e-mail it to the ranch. But he'd wanted to see Alexander's reaction to Josie, and hers to him. He wanted to know what kind of emotion lingered between the two of them.

Even more, he had wanted to get Josie out of the house. He'd wanted to get her in the sun, give her a change of scenery. She'd taken to working with Imogene all day, vacuuming and cooking and arranging flowers. It was as if she felt she needed to earn her keep, which was absurd. He wanted her to relax, and enjoy herself for a change.

But she didn't look relaxed. She stared through the windshield toward the sales center, her hands braided in her lap.

They'd confirmed that Alexander was working this afternoon. A one-hour drive was too far for a wild-goose chase. He might be in one of the model homes, shepherding a customer, but he might be just on the other side of that carved fake-mission door.

"If he does turn out to be…Flim, I wonder what he'll do when he sees me?" She glanced at Chase. "Especially when he sees me standing next to the real Chase Clayton?"

"Well…" He smiled. "Have you ever seen when Popeye gets surprised, and his eyes bulge out of their sockets? He lifts off the ground, and his hat shoots off his head?"

"You think so?" She chuckled. "I don't know. When we were together, Flim was considerably smoother than that."

He grinned, ridiculously pleased with himself for being able to make her laugh.

"Of course he was smooth. He'd have to be, or no one would believe he was me."

She groaned. "Luckily, he didn't have to pretend to be humble." She took a deep breath, then pushed open the truck door. "All right, I'm as ready as I'll ever be. Let's get the Father Hunt started."

The sales center was packed. According to the newspaper advertisement blown up and displayed on an easel by the door, this was the final day of the preconstruction sale prices.

He started to make a joke about that, but he realized that, under his arm, her shoulders trembled slightly.

He looked down at her face, which had grown almost as pale as it had been when he first saw her. Alexander was nowhere in sight, so that wasn't it. It was obviously just the fear of seeing him.

She was dreading this more than he'd realized.

He wished he knew exactly why. Was it because seeing Flim would hurt too badly? Or was it because so much was riding on

Flim's willingness to accept financial responsibility for this child?

If it was just about the money, she could relax. If Alexander turned out to be the father, Chase would see to it that he did the right thing, even if it meant choking every damn dollar out of the bastard, one penny at a time.

"Do you see him?" She was walking gingerly, as if she were balancing an egg on the crown of her head.

"Not yet." Several salesmen wearing forest-green blazers with name tags glided around, each of them with a customer in tow. But no Alexander. Chase hadn't seen his cousin in years, but he would recognize that ambitious, ingratiating face anywhere.

It was so like his own and yet, he hoped, so different.

He guided Josie over to the architectural model that dominated the center of the large room. It was quite elaborate, with small fake trees and people, and even a couple of dogs. Maybe it would distract her.

"Look," he said calmly. "The development is going to be even bigger than the picture in the brochure."

She nodded, though he wasn't sure she heard him. She gripped the edge of the table with both hands, and he noticed that her knuckles were white.

"Hello, there. I'm Patty. I'd be glad to answer any questions you might have." A young woman in one of the green blazers stood beside Josie. "Would you like to tour one of the models?"

Josie looked up blankly, as if she weren't sure how to handle this departure from their script.

Chase put his arm around Josie, smiling at the woman. "Thanks, but we're waiting for Alexander Clayton. You don't happen to know where he is, do you?"

She tapped her pen against her lips. "Let's see. He was with a customer a little while ago. I think they may have gone to one of the—"

She broke off, her eyes brightening. "Oh, there he is. He's coming in the door right now."

Chase felt Josie stiffen. He tightened his arm around her shoulders. "I'm here," he said, though he wasn't sure that would help.

They watched the entryway in silence. For a minute, all they could see of Alexander was his arm. He was holding the door open with one hand, while he stood on the sidewalk, no doubt giving a last-minute pep talk to his customers.

Buy today, or else...

Finally, he waved them off and moved into the building, his face still beaming from all that energetic salesmanship. He scanned the room with his bright blue eyes, trying to pick out the most likely buyers.

Chase felt irrationally ticked off, just watching him. He looked handsome as hell, full of life and confidence. Several women in the room smiled at him as he moved through the crowd.

Chase looked at Josie. She shook her head numbly.

"No," she said, frowning. "No."

"He's not the one?"

"No."

"Are you sure?"

She nodded. "Of course I'm sure. Do you think I wouldn't recognize the man I—"

"Chase?" Alexander's prowl for well-heeled customers had brought him close enough to recognize his cousin. "Chase, is that you?"

He moved toward them, his trim body dapper in his blazer, his clear, broad brow furrowed with surprise. He was clearly shocked to see Chase here. And a little defiant, too, perhaps—daring Chase to bring up their uncomfortable past. Chase could see him trying to decide whether to extend a hand, just in case it was rejected.

Then, at the last minute, Alexander noticed Josie. Chase caught the quick dart of his cousin's eyes down to her breasts, the rapid-fire appraisal of her body. She was too thin, but she had curves in all the right places, and Alexander no doubt liked what he saw.

So the bastard hadn't changed. He was still a hound dog, interested in only one thing. Make that two things. Sex and money. He was still hungry for more of each. And if he could take them from Chase, all the better.

Surprise, defiance, greed, envy… Chase saw all that in the two seconds it took Alexander to reach them. He knew his cousin well, and had always found him easy to read.

But the one thing he'd expected to see wasn't anywhere in sight.

He didn't see guilt.

Nope. The Father Hunt didn't end here.

JOSIE HAD NEVER BEEN to San Antonio before, so when they finished the perfunctory tour of Alexander's model homes, Chase decided to take her to dinner at Riverwalk.

It was just the thing, Chase said, to clear away any unpleasant taste left by the tacky Olde Mission Woods—or by Alexander himself.

He was right. It was lovely. The retail-restaurant wonderland built along the banks of the San Antonio River was a magical spot at night, filled with light and color, with the scents of fabulous food and the lilting guitars of street performers.

They ate wonderful Mexican cuisine under a blue umbrella and watched the people strolling along the curved paths, holding hands and laughing, sometimes spontaneously breaking into song. Platform boats floated down the river, stirring up the reflected lights, until the whole river seemed a swirling cauldron of color.

"Oh, my heavens," she said when she finished the last bite of her taco salad. She leaned back and put both hands against her stomach. "I think I'm going to pop."

"Me, too." He leaned forward. "But no queasiness?"

She shook her head. The morning sickness seemed to have passed. "I'm feeling great."

"Good. Come on, then. Let's walk it off."

She looked longingly at the winding trails, bursting with greenery and flowers. Then she looked at her watch. "You don't think we should be getting back? I know you have to be up early tomorrow for that meeting and the auction."

"Hang tomorrow," he said. "I can sleep through the meeting if I have to. The night is gorgeous, and the company is great. I feel as if I'm finally getting to know the real Josie. No, ma'am. I'm not giving up a minute of tonight."

She knew he wasn't just being polite. Somehow, after getting through the meeting with Alexander, she'd felt a surge of well-being and confidence, and it had made her feel like herself again.

All this contentment didn't make any sense, really. Nothing had been resolved. Alexander had been eliminated, but they'd just have to resume the hunt tomorrow— and who knew where it might lead them?

For now, though, she'd cleared the hurdle. And somehow, that seemed to give her the freedom to let go and relax.

This kind of camaraderie wouldn't have seemed possible, back when she first arrived, hurt and embarrassed and frightened. But little by little, mostly because of Chase's easy nature, they'd become... well, almost friends.

Sometimes, after Imogene had gone to bed, Josie and Chase sat out on the back porch at night, listening to the owls call and the wind rustling in the trees. Sometimes, they talked over the problem of finding Flim, Chase asking questions and Josie trying to remember something, anything, that would lead to an identification. But sometimes, bored with Flim, they'd wander off to other topics, problems on the ranch, a horse he was thinking of buying, or something she was reading for school.

She enjoyed those quiet nights. Almost too much. He was interesting and witty, but comfortably down-to-earth. No airs, no vanity, no subtle reminders that he was a Clayton, and she was just his uninvited guest.

But she didn't need reminders. How could she forget? For twenty-five thousand acres all around them, the owls they listened to, and the trees they perched in, belonged to him.

Tonight, though, out here on neutral ground, all that fell away. Tonight they were just two people having dinner. Equal partners in a quest to find the truth.

She could still remember the warmth of his protective arm, resting against her shoulders, as she turned to face Alexander. She could still hear the bracing strength of his voice, assuring her that he was there, that she wasn't alone.

In that moment, something had changed. The mousy Cinderella had dropped away, and Josie had been reborn.

They'd sat over dinner for almost three hours, and the conversation had flowed as easily as the river beside them. It was strangely exciting, and she felt that she could keep talking all night.

He stood, and held out his hand. "Come."

"Okay," she said, pushing her chair back. "But I hope you don't regret it, especially if you end up buying some nasty nag at the auction because you were too groggy to think straight."

"I promise you." He took her hand. "I won't regret it."

They walked slowly, taking in the beauty

of the place. Shining bridges looped and braided the pedestrian walkways on both sides of the water. The cafés glowed green and yellow and red and blue, and white fairy lights draped from one awning to the next, as if magical spiders had woven enchanted webs of stars.

He had let go of her hand, but on the narrow pedestrian walk they strolled so close together their shoulders often touched.

"You seem to be in a mighty good mood," she observed when he tossed a twenty-dollar bill into the open guitar case of a street performer.

"I am. I have to admit I'm glad Alexander didn't turn out to be the guy we're looking for."

"Why?"

Yesterday, she wouldn't have dared to ask that question. She would have assumed that he didn't want the baby's father to be part of his family because he didn't want to be tied permanently to her in any way.

Tonight she knew better. They might be from different tax brackets, but she wasn't exactly a pariah, and he wasn't a superficial snob.

"Why? Because he's a weasel."

She laughed. "I think it's pretty much guaranteed that whoever pretended to be you is a weasel, don't you? At best."

"I guess. But Alexander is a particularly annoying weasel." He glanced at her. "You aren't disappointed, are you? Believe me, he would make a terrible father."

"No. Not disappointed, exactly."

"Then what?"

She tried to pinpoint how she felt. "Maybe it's just that Alexander would have been a known quantity. He's not an escapee from a lunatic asylum, or the Boston Strangler. And his motive for impersonating you would be relatively benign. A lifelong envy of his glamorous cousin, Chase, who's always had all the luck."

He grimaced. "Doesn't sound very benign to me. Still sounds criminal—and cruel."

"Well, it's not nearly as creepy as some total stranger deciding to steal your name, your life, your childhood memories. Right down to Yipster, the world's nicest dog."

He seemed to be taking it in. "Yeah," he said finally. "I guess you're right. But I honestly don't think you have to worry about Flim turning out to be the Boston Strangler."

"Why not?"

He smiled. "I think your instincts would have warned you to stay away. I just can't see you falling for someone who was truly evil."

"You may have more confidence in me than I have in myself," she said. She paused to watch one of the crowded platform boats go by. "But I hope you're right."

The boat seemed to be filled with couples, some older, some still in their teens. Arms entwined, heads tilted together, they snuggled and stared at the stars.

It was that kind of night. Balmy, beautiful, heavy with the scent of flowers.

Even the walkway where they stood was full of paired-off lovers. One young family had also stopped to watch the boat. The man wore a soft fabric baby carrier that held his infant up against his chest. His wife leaned her head against his shoulder, her hand cupping the baby's tiny head.

The love around the three of them was so powerful it practically glowed like one of the Riverwalk spotlights. They seemed wrapped in a magic circle of joy—and Josie was sure they weren't even aware of anyone else around them.

Suddenly, the painful truth of her situation hit her like a dart, right between the ribs. She would never have any of that. She and her baby's father would never stand inside a magic cocoon of love, never feel three hearts beating as one.

"Are you all right?"

She tore her gaze away from the little family. "I'm fine," she said.

But it wasn't true. The comfortable peace that had buoyed her for the past three hours drained away as if someone had pulled an invisible plug. She sagged, inexplicably tired, and for the first time she noticed that the river smelled slightly musty and stale.

"Are you tired?" He touched her elbow. "I've kept you out too long."

"No, no, it's been terrific, honestly."

At that moment, the baby lifted its head uncertainly, wobbling with the charming weakness of a newborn, and let out a sleepy, mewing cry. His parents smiled at one another, then bent over him, murmuring the eternal wordless promises of love.

Chase clearly hadn't noticed them before. He watched for a second, until the baby settled back into his papoose, lips pursing and unpursing. The infant shut his unfocused eyes and sighed, breathing in the security of his father's scent.

Then Chase turned to Josie, his face tight.

"It's going to be all right," he said. "I promise you. It's going to be all right."

It was the same tone, the same soothing nonsense the young father was even now crooning to his baby.

She nodded, trying to smile. "I know," she said.

He put the flat of his hand against her cheek. She felt her head tilt into it, just a fraction of an inch, as if of its own accord,

Her eyes drifted shut. His hands were

warm. And strong. His thumb traced the ridge of her cheekbone, grazed the sensitive edge of her ear.

"Josie."

She opened her eyes. He was gazing down at her, the blue of his eyes drowned by the night. She couldn't read them.

But she knew he could read hers.

He hesitated another agonizing second, and then he kissed her. Slowly. And so softly that, at first, it was no more than the tingle of heat. Warm streaks of that glittering warmth cascaded down across her shoulders, across her back, over her breasts.

She made a small sound. She felt as weak as an infant herself, falling into a warm, deep dream of Chase.

"Josie," he whispered again, right against her lips.

And then he pulled back. He blinked, as if he were trying to awaken from a trance.

He let his hand fall from her cheek.

"We should go home," he said.

CHAPTER TEN

THE RIDE HOME WAS QUIET, the empty road stretching out like a bleached ribbon in the moonlight. He turned on the radio, found a nice soft rock station and dialed the volume just high enough to discourage talking. What the devil would they say? He did *not* intend to talk about that kiss, and it would have felt totally fake to talk about anything else.

He shouldn't have worried. Josie seemed as determined as he was to pretend the kiss hadn't happened. Besides, she was obviously exhausted, and within ten minutes she'd nodded off, her head tilted against the side window.

That left Chase with an hour and fifty minutes of pure solitude, to lecture himself for being such a goddamn fool.

The highway lights flashed rhythmically against her face, first spotlighting, then obscuring that sweet mouth, those long, dark lashes. *Now you see her, now you don't.* It kept Chase's nerves on edge, to the point that he had to make an effort not to look.

He searched for a country station. But some guy was singing about lips sweeter than wine, a cliché Chase had always found particularly dumb. But he realized that the guy who first wrote that line had probably kissed someone like Josie Whitford.

He turned to public radio instead, but they were playing some cello thing fit only for a funeral. With a disgusted grunt, he flicked the radio off completely.

As if the silence reached her dreams, she sighed, wriggling into a more comfortable position. A delicate finger of her perfume reached out and touched him on the nose.

God, would he never make it back to the Double C? He'd traveled this road a hundred times, but it hadn't ever seemed so long. The white lines kept rolling under his tires, but new ones continued to slide at him, unwound from an endless string of torture.

And—damn it. When the car finally dragged itself through the Double C gates, he realized that, for him at least, the night wasn't over.

Trent was waiting for them, a dark silhouette on the brightly lit front porch. The minute the truck came to a stop, crunching across the oyster-shell driveway, he loped over to the driver's side.

Chase was already rolling down the window. Trent didn't have any mother hen tendencies. If he'd waited up for Chase, there was a damn good reason.

Or rather, a damn bad one.

"It's Captain Kirk," Trent said in a low voice, resting his elbows on the window and leaning in. "He showed signs of colic this afternoon, and tonight he started rolling. Johnson is with him. He's hurting pretty bad, I think."

Chase cursed under his breath. "Have you called Doc Blaiser?"

"Of course. He was at the Berringer place. He'll be here in about fifteen minutes."

On the other side of the truck, Josie was finally waking up. She rubbed her eyes and moistened her dry lips. She ran her fingers through her tousled hair and blinked toward Chase.

"I'm sorry," she said around a yawn. "I guess I was more tired than I thought." Then she noticed Trent at the window. She must have seen something on his face, because her smile died. "What's wrong?"

"One of my horses is sick. Colic. It's probably nothing, but you can't mess around with colic."

"Which horse?"

He frowned. He'd forgotten that she already knew most of his horses by name. It crossed his mind suddenly that her collection of "Chase" stories might hold a clue. How current was Flim's information? If they could determine when he stopped having access to details about Chase's private life, they might be able to pinpoint how long ago Chase had known him.

For instance, Alexander wouldn't have known about any horses Chase bought in the past five years. Charming Billy had been gone for three.

But that was something Chase and Josie could explore tomorrow.

"It's Captain Kirk," he told her. He turned back to Trent. "When did the rolling start?"

"I'm not sure." Trent's face tightened. "Eli was supposed to be sitting with him. When I came through to check on things, maybe an hour ago, Captain Kirk was already on the ground, in a lot of pain. But Eli wasn't there."

"What?"

"I know."

"Where the hell was he?"

"We just found him. Out behind the hay barn. He and Nikki were...counting stars."

"Unbelievable."

"Yeah. I told him to take her home and then get his ass back here so that you can chew it off."

Chase pressed his fingers against the

bridge of his nose, trying to hold back the headache that had begun to set up shop in his skull.

"I haven't got the energy." He exhaled. "Just fire him."

Trent nodded. "Gladly."

Beside him, Josie made a small noise.

Chase turned to her. "I've got to get to the stables," he said. "Are you okay?"

"Yes, I'm fine. It's just that…you're really going to fire that boy?"

"Yes. This isn't his first mistake, although this one would be enough by itself. You don't leave a sick animal alone, not on this ranch. But as it happens, he broke a twenty-thousand-dollar mechanical cow earlier this week. So this screwup is actually his second big one."

"Third," Trent put in. "He's ignored the feed schedule, fed the horses early or late, to work it around his social life. Probably all week."

"Oh." On hearing that, Josie looked subdued.

Chase wondered if she knew enough

about horses to understand how imperative it was to establish and keep a regular feeding routine. Or maybe she was just remembering a few days ago, when she had challenged him about giving up on the roan with a phobia.

She really did have a thing for protecting the underdog, didn't she?

Trent glanced at Josie through the window. He raised one brow to Chase. "You sure you want to fire him?"

"No," Chase said. "What I *want* to do is strangle him." He opened the truck door and climbed out. "Get Josie upstairs, Trent. And then tell Eli Breslin to get his lazy, undisciplined butt off my ranch."

"Sue, come on! Please! You could make him change his mind."

Nicole, dressed in the trashiest short-shorts Susannah had ever seen, had been pacing the wood-paneled great room at Everly Ranch for the past ten minutes.

She dropped onto the arm of the big leather sofa, then popped right back up again. She was clearly too full of furious adrenaline to settle anywhere. "You know you could get Eli his job back. You just don't want to!"

"You're right," Susannah said, putting her initials on the housekeeper's shopping list, then turning to the menu for the Burn Center's barn dance this weekend—their biggest fund-raiser of the year.

Nikki, who had already opened her mouth for her next barrage of accusations, stared at her sister. "What did you say?"

"I said you're right. I don't want to. Chase knows how to run his own ranch, and he wouldn't welcome any interference from me, any more than I'd welcome interference about Everly from him."

"But you're his fiancée!" Nikki's voice had reached a high-pitched whine. She sounded about ten years old, which made her thick, black eyeliner look even more absurd. "Doesn't that mean anything?"

"It means I respect him enough to leave him alone. What you and Eli did last night was wrong. You know it, and Eli knows it.

It was selfish of you to let him put his job in jeopardy. Not to mention what could have happened to Captain Kirk."

That took a little of the wind out of Nikki's sails. She loved the sweet old bay. Chase had taught her to ride on Captain Kirk's gentle, slightly swaying back.

But apparently teenage hormones were even more powerful than old loyalties. "Captain Kirk was fine when Eli left him. And he wasn't gone that long. Trent tried to make it sound worse than it was."

"How could he? Eli had a job to do, and he didn't do it. End of story."

"You think it's that simple?" Nikki's face was as red as her midriff-cropped see-through-net shirt. "God, you're all such hypocrites and liars!"

Susannah half rose from her chair. She felt a shocking desire to slap her little sister silly. How dare she take that tone? But she lowered herself back onto the cushion, fighting for control.

"Nicole, if you are going to be insolent, this conversation is over."

"Why can't you at least tell the truth? Chase didn't fire Eli because he left the barn. He fired him because you asked him to."

Tears were rolling down her cheeks, and she wiped them with the hem of her tacky shirt. "You wanted Chase to get rid of him. Just because you're so miserable, you can't stand to see me happy."

Oh, *right*. Susannah dropped the menu on her desk and rubbed her temples. God bless the egocentricity of youth. Your relationship hits a snag, and the whole world must be in a conspiracy against True Love.

"That's absurd," she said wearily. "I'm not miserable, and even if I were, I'd still want you to be happy."

"You're not miserable? Look at you. You never have any fun. You never do anything but worry about the ranch and making money. On the weekends, your *entertainment* is working at the Burn Center."

"That's not called misery, Nikki. It's called growing up. Someday you'll learn that you can't be happy if you're ignoring your obligations."

"God, Susannah. Can you hear yourself? You sound just like Grandfather."

That was a jab right at the jugular, and Nikki knew it. In their family, comparing people to Arlington Everly was like comparing them to Hitler, or Satan.

Susannah glanced at the portrait over the fireplace, which her grandfather had commissioned just a few years ago, right before he died. The hard brown eyes met hers without wavering, and without mercy, just as they had done in life.

Arlington had refused to smile for the sitting. He had prohibited the artist to indulge in any sugarcoating, any prettying-up, to make him look younger, nicer, less thin-lipped and hollow-eyed. Less like a man about to die.

He'd been proud of being the toughest son of a bitch in East Texas. He thought every crag and furrow in his strong-boned, weathered face was a badge of honor. Stone-jawed and sour, clearly at the emaciated end of his rugged life, he stood beneath a rack of sixteen-point antlers, the biggest kill of his eighty-nine years.

Death comes for the hunter. And the hunter doesn't flinch.

"Maybe I am like him," Susannah said dully. "Maybe I have to be."

"Okay, then, fine." Nikki curled her lip and glared at her sister with scornful green eyes that could have been cloned from the man in the portrait.

Susannah braced herself. Nikki clearly knew she'd hit a brick wall and being thwarted made her mean. *She* was like her grandfather that way.

Maybe, each in her own style, they'd both inherited his hard-hearted streak.

"So I guess if I want help I should ask Josie Whitford, I'll bet Chase listens to her. At least she looks like a real person. Like someone who might have a heart. Because *you* clearly don't."

MID MORNING, while Josie was doing her English homework, Chase stuck his head in briefly to let her know Captain Kirk was fine. Apparently, though they'd feared enteritis, it had turned out to be plain old gas. Painful, but not dangerous.

He looked relieved, and she was happy for him. Apparently, no matter how many younger, more valuable quarter horses they bought for this ranch, he'd always have a special affection for that old bay.

He didn't stay long. He had an appointment in town, he said.

They didn't mention Eli Breslin. Josie had immediately regretted her remarks last night—and her embarrassment had kept her awake. Round about midnight, she'd actually considered putting on a robe and going out to the stables to apologize.

But then she realized she was just kidding herself. The apology was secondary. Mostly, she just wanted to go out there because Chase was out there.

Had she hoped he'd kiss her again?

Surely not. It had been a wonderful kiss. But they both knew it was a mistake they must never repeat. So she stayed where she was and willed herself to sleep.

After he left, she spent the rest of the morning in his office, using his computer to upload her homework and take the weekly vocab quiz. Thank heavens for online classes! Otherwise, she might have had to let that Greyhound bus drag her back to Riverfork after all.

But, now that she'd been fired from the Not Guilty Café, she had no reason to hurry home. Online banking took care of the bills. Online education kept her enrolled in the one class she'd been able to afford. She didn't own a dog or a cat or a parakeet. Not even a goldfish was staring sadly at the door, praying for her to turn the key.

Which was a good thing. Because every day she saw a little more clearly just how much she didn't want to return to her old life. If you could call it a life. A half-empty efficiency apartment, an online class and a job waiting tables hadn't ever seemed exciting, but she had accepted it as the slow road to something better.

Now she knew it wasn't enough.

Not for her. And not for the baby who would be born in September.

What she didn't see clearly was what she *did* want. And unfortunately she'd have to decide before long. That bill she'd clicked this morning, sending in her quarterly health insurance premium, had scraped the last of the cash from the bottom of the barrel.

She was going to have to get a job and very soon.

Even if she had a huge, cushiony savings account, she couldn't take advantage of Chase's hospitality forever. No matter what he said about teaming up to find the bad guy, this lovely interlude was nothing but a charity vacation at Club Clayton.

Lazy mornings, catered food, long walks beneath flowering trees. Horses gamboling in green pastures. Daffodils dancing at the edge of Clayton Creek. A handsome, intelligent man to drive her to the doctor, pick up her medicines, sit across from her at dinner.

Kiss her in the moonlight...

If she wasn't careful, this delightful fantasy would spoil her for real life.

It was time to climb back onto her own two feet. Thanks to Chase and his doctors, thanks to Imogene and her fabulous feasts...and of course, thanks to the insulin pump, she was healthy enough to get back to work.

Healthier, in fact, than she'd been in months. Maybe years.

Tomorrow, she'd look in the paper and see what jobs were listed nearby. Why not move east? This part of Texas was beautiful. After only ten days here, the three years she'd spent in dusty Riverfork seemed like a bad dream.

Besides, her mother and stepfather lived in Austin. When the baby was born, wouldn't it be nice to have family close by?

She clicked off the monitor and stood, setting her papers to one side. Now she really was dreaming. She could see her stepfather's face, if she asked him to make room in his well-run life for an unwed mother and her illegitimate baby. He'd trot out some judgmental cliché that let him off the hook entirely. Josie had made her own bed, he'd insist, and she would have to lie in it alone.

Her mother would probably wish she could patch things up. She might yearn to be a part of her grandchild's life. She might even send Josie a twenty-dollar bill in the mail, or a gift certificate to a sensible drugstore.

But she wouldn't have the nerve to cross her husband. She never had.

Outside, a mower was humming along, happily munching on the grass that had shot up after last night's rain.

Josie went to the window, but Chase's truck wasn't there. He hadn't come back after his appointment. She wondered if he was avoiding her.

She needed something to distract her. She made her way back to the kitchen, as usual following her nose.

Imogene looked more frazzled than Josie had ever seen her, her wispy hair flying all around her face, and her chip-munk cheeks flushed beet-red.

"Oh, Lordy, I hope you've come to help."

Josie smiled. Here in the kitchen with Imogene was just about the only time she didn't feel like a freeloader. With no fuss or bother, Imogene always put her to work.

"I have. What do you need?"

"I need someone to take these box lunches out to the construction site. Can you drive?"

Josie wrinkled her nose. "That depends on who you ask. The guy who fixed the pillar out front probably doesn't think so."

Imogene waved her hand impatiently. "I mean when you're not in a diabetic coma."

"Yes," Josie said. "That is, I could, if I had anything left to drive."

"Oh, we've got vehicles all over the ranch, just sitting there growing moss. But my sister is coming in from Houston, and I've got to meet her at the airport in an hour. I'm running behind, and I need you to take these lunches out to the site."

"Okay. I'd be glad to."

Imogene hadn't even waited for her response. She was already drawing a crude map on the back of a napkin. "It's not far. Just come out here—" she pointed to an intersection nearby "—and then turn right. It's the old Bradley place, about six miles past Everly. It burned down last month, and they're holding a barn raising, so to speak."

"Who is?"

"Everybody," she said absently. She was counting boxes under her breath, pointing and scowling, as if someone might be trying to fool her into sending the wrong amounts.

Finally satisfied, she turned to Josie. "Take one of the vans, so it'll all fit. The red ones are Black Forest ham and Swiss on croissant. The yellow ones are mandarin chicken salad. The white ones are grilled eggplant."

"Yummy," Josie said sincerely. She'd had one of Imogene's grilled eggplant sandwiches, and it was heaven.

"You get any complaints, you just tell them to shut up and eat." She wiped a strand of hair away from her damp forehead. "Ned had the nerve to ask for a turkey wrap, can you believe it? I said, you get what you always get. If I give in to even one person, I'll end up making forty different sandwiches for forty different mouths."

"Do they have barn raisings a lot?"

"This one's organized by the Burn Center. But about once a month, they're out there fixing something for somebody. Like the Habitat people, only more informal like. Chase's mother started it, but now it's just a habit. It's the way Chase is. He likes to help people out."

"Yes," Josie said, nodding self-consciously. "I know."

Imogene laughed, reaching around to untie her apron. "Lordie, honey, I didn't mean you. You're..." She screwed up her mouth, considering. "You're different."

"I am?"

"Yes. Now get going. You've got to stop by the diner, too, and I won't be sending soggy sandwiches."

CHAPTER ELEVEN

AFTER THE BLOWUP with Nikki, Susannah was almost too distracted to focus on anything. As she pulled into the Bradley lot, with her forty-two-ounce jugs of lemonade, coffee and ice water on the seat beside her, she was still reliving the argument, thinking of all the brilliant comebacks she should have used.

The whole thing made her furious, and her body thrummed with tension. As a result, her foot was heavy on the pedals, and she was going far too fast. She took the corner too sharply.

And she came within a rabbit's whisker of colliding with another car, pulling in from the other side.

The Coleman jugs tumbled everywhere

as she hit the brakes. Her head snapped forward, and she felt the cool kiss of the windshield against her brow. She squeezed her eyes shut, waiting for the sound of shattering glass.

But nothing happened. The other car braked sharply, too. Her shoulder belt held her in place. The car rocked slightly, settling, like a cup knocked sideways, but not hard enough to fall over.

She closed her eyes and tried to breathe. Gradually, over a couple of seconds, she felt her own balance returning. The whooshing in her ears stopped as the adrenaline eased off. As shock receded, she gained a little room in her brain to think.

And that's when she noticed that the shiny black Mercedes she'd almost hit belonged to Trent.

Damn it. Could anything else go wrong today?

He recovered faster than she did and pulled his car smoothly into one of the few open slots. They were late for the building party, and everyone else clearly had already arrived.

If only she'd come sooner.

If only he hadn't come at all.

He got out, and sauntered back toward her, his movements efficient and graceful. He was never awkward, was he? She felt an unwanted response to the elegant motion of his perfectly shaped body. But she couldn't help that. He was a good-looking man, and she still had eyes in her head.

However, she didn't have to let herself stare. She averted her gaze and focused on maneuvering her car into the only other available space. When she turned in, she found herself nose to nose with Chase's truck. It felt comforting, like encountering an ally just before a battle.

If only Chase were in it, and could act as a buffer between his two friends. It was a role he'd perfected over the past few years.

But Chase had probably already been working on the Bradley house for hours.

Oh, well. What couldn't be avoided might as well be faced. It was no big deal, really. She saw Trent all the time, though she hadn't seen him since her engagement to Chase had been announced.

Even before that, they had always managed to avoid being alone.

She took a deep breath, grabbed one of the coolers and climbed out. It was a hot, sunny day already. Everyone would be dying of thirst, wondering where the drinks were.

"I'm sorry," she said as Trent approached her. "That was my fault."

"It certainly was," he said with that air of amusement that attracted so many women, but only irritated her. "Did you learn that trick from Josie? I thought I was having déjà vu for a minute there."

His gaze scanned her lazily. "Are you all right?"

"I'm fine." Her knees wobbled a little— the adrenaline, no doubt—so she stood by the side of the car, waiting for them to settle. "The lemonade is probably going to have a nice head of froth, though."

He peered in. The jugs lay every which

way on the floor of the passenger seat. "I'll get the rest of those for you."

She shook her head. "I'm all right, thanks. Chase will get them."

Trent raised one of his dark brows. "Chase is probably fifteen feet in the air right now, with a mouth full of carpenter's nails. You'd drag him over here, just to deny me the privilege of hauling your lemonade?"

She flushed. Through the years, she'd developed a thick skin where Trent was concerned, and it ordinarily took more than his sardonic smile to fluster her. But she simply wasn't up to sparring with him today, not after going toe-to-toe with Nikki all morning.

"Of course not," she said. "If you think it's such a big deal to carry the coolers, help yourself. I'm just—" She backed away to provide access to the car. "I'm just surprised to see you here, that's all. You don't usually…I mean, when the Burn Center is involved in something—"

He shrugged. "Bradley is a friend of mine. I want to help him. The fact that he ended up in your precious Burn Center doesn't change that."

She felt her spine stiffen. "My precious Burn Center?"

She shouldn't have provided the opening for him. She should have seen that he was spoiling for a fight.

"Sure it is. It's your baby, isn't it? You spearheaded the drive for it, you raised the money for it, and you've been martyring yourself for it ever since. St. Susannah of the Fiery Flames, that's what we call you."

She put the cooler of lemonade down carefully. And then she reached out and slapped him. Hard. Flat-palmed across the cheek.

With lightning reflexes, he caught her hand. He held it in the air, his gaze never dropping from hers, even as the red outline of her fingers appeared like a brand on his face.

"How dare you?" Her breath came roughly. She refused to demean herself by trying to wriggle her hand away. He was twice as strong as she was, and she wouldn't be free until he decided to let her go.

"How dare I? I dare because it's true. And because enough is enough. It's gone on too long, Sue. It's been more than ten years. More than a decade since Paul died. And you're still using that goddamn Burn Center to punish me for it."

"That's ridiculous." She lifted her chin. "But how typical of you to think that everything, including a project I've been deeply involved in for years, is actually all about you."

"It is all about me. Or rather, it's all about *us*."

"Us?" She laughed harshly. "There hasn't been an 'us' for ten years, Trent. And there never will be again."

He let go of her hand slowly. His face looked raw, shockingly young, stripped of the mocking mask that had covered it for so long. She caught the faint whiff of old smoke in the air. Was it left over from the Bradley fire, she wondered? Or was it the smell of her own bridges burning?

"What the hell happened to you, Sue? You used to be so…" He shook his head, as if he found himself unable to come up with the right word. "So…"

She held her breath, calling on her hard-won thick skin to protect her from whatever he might say next. To keep her from doing anything stupid, like letting her voice break, or allowing a tear to fall.

He gave up. "When did you turn so cold?"

"I don't know. Maybe it was during the six months I sat in Paul's hospital room, watching him die. Watching his mother's heart break. Watching his father fade away before my eyes."

Trent shook his head again. It was a primitive denial, a subconscious rejection of a truth too painful to accept. But it was all true. Why shouldn't he face it? She'd had to face it back then, day after day, month after month. And she faced it still, every day, in her memories, in her dreams.

She shrugged. "Or maybe it was the day your father showed up and told me you were gone. That you'd left town. And you'd married someone else."

"You know why I left. Surely you

haven't forgotten telling me you'd never speak to me again as long as you lived."

"No, I haven't forgotten. So you moved on. And quickly, too. Well, good for you. It shows a certain resilience, to be able to kill a man, abandon your family and betray your girlfriend, all without blinking an eye."

"What is it you won't forgive me for, Sue? Is it what happened to Paul? Or is it the fact that I married someone else?"

"Hey, guys." Suddenly Chase was there behind them, looking sweaty and golden from hard labor in the spring sun. Her heart was pounding like a jackhammer. It amazed her that anyone could look so wholesome, so normal, at a moment like this.

"What's going on out here?" Chase frowned at Trent, then turned his gaze to Susannah. "Is everything all right?"

Susannah looked at Trent, inviting him to respond. In an instant, his elegant bitterness was back in place. He was devilishly handsome, dangerously self-composed and utterly unreachable.

"Not to worry, Chase," he said, pulling

his keys from his pocket. He shook them with a light jingle. "I was just leaving."

"Damn it, Trent, what have you—" He narrowed his eyes, obviously spotting the shape of Susannah's hand still flaming on the other man's cheek. He whipped his head around. "Sue? Tell me. Are you okay?"

"Okay?" Trent laughed, a jagged, joyless sound. "No, she's not okay. She's a stone-cold bitch, and there's nothing that remotely resembles a heart beating inside that beautiful breast."

"Cripes, Trent—"

"Sorry, buddy." He smiled at Chase with his usual ironic detachment. "But it's true. And all I can say is…better you than me."

THE SLOW HANDS DINER was easy to find, thank goodness. Josie parked the van out front, locked the precious boxed lunches inside, and then hurried to the front counter.

A huge man ambled over. He had bushy black hair, horn-rims, and a tattoo on his monstrous bicep that said Sell by: 1987.

"Hi, there," he said with a smile so warm it took her by surprise. "Lunch for one?"

"No, thanks. Imogene asked me to tell you that she needs two of your big muddies. And she said, well, she said we're in a bit of a hurry."

Actually, Imogene had said to tell him to "hustle like it's 1970," but at the last minute Josie just couldn't do it.

"Two big muddies coming up." The giant reached under the counter, grabbed a bottled water and handed it to her. "Grab a stool and make yourself at home. I'll be back in two shakes of a stick."

She took the stool closest to the cash register. It was the best vantage point for seeing the dozen or so customers, all dusty, stubbled ranch hands who were clearly stretching their lunch hours to the max.

Slow Hands... She smiled to herself, finally getting the pun.

She unscrewed the cap of the water and, taking a drink, sneaked a glance at the first table. She didn't really think that Flim could be one of these customers—he had been so well-groomed, so believable in the role of a privileged young son of Texas. But you never knew. Give some of these guys good clothes and a good haircut, and they might look like Robert Redford themselves.

She checked each table out, one sip of water per cowboy. But when the bottle came up empty, so did her search. Flim wasn't here.

Then she noticed that the walls were crowded with photographs. Rodeos, it looked like, and county fairs, and Fourth of July picnics.

A gold mine...a virtual mug book of local cowboys.

She slid off her stool and walked casually over to the nearest photo. It showed several cowboys in ten-gallon hats, grinning as they gathered around a beautiful black horse. Mysty Rios takes the blue rosette in reining, the caption read.

But she didn't recognize any of the men in the picture. She tried not to feel disappointed. Even bothering to look at the pictures was a little like playing the lottery.

Actually, the odds that she'd find Flim's face among this sea of cowboys were probably even slimmer than her odds of winning the Saturday-night jackpot.

But here she was, with time to kill, and it didn't hurt to try. How she would love to be able to walk up to Chase and say, "I found him!"

She smiled at one of the real-life ranch hands as she bumped his chair, trying to get a better angle on the picture on the wall behind him. "Sorry," she said. "I just wanted to take a quick look—"

"Miss Whitford?" The cowboy stood up awkwardly and took his hat in his hand. "Boss Johnson," he supplied politely. "I work at the Double C."

She searched her mind, and then she placed him. He was the cutting horse trainer, the one who had spotted the phobia in that beautiful roan.

"Hi, Mr. Johnson. I'm sorry I didn't recognize you."

If only he knew *how* sorry. When she'd seen Johnson riding the roan, he'd reminded her of Willie Nelson, his face covered in a reddish-gray beard, and his hair tied back in a long, scruffy ponytail. Today he had apparently come from the barber. His face was clean-shaven, and he had the neatly parted, above-the-ears haircut of a banker, or a schoolteacher.

It was unnerving to realize how much of her impressions were based on such superficial details. If she couldn't recognize a man she'd seen just a few days ago, a man who wasn't trying to hide from anyone, how could she be so sure she'd know Flim when she saw him?

"It's okay, ma'am," Johnson said with a smile. "I reckon my own mother wouldn't recognize me today. I'm fixing to ask my girl to marry me, and I thought I'd better not show up looking like yesterday's hog slop."

"You look great. How romantic. I'll keep my fingers crossed that she says yes."

"Oh, she will." Johnson laughed, a big, heartfelt roll from the diaphragm. "She's been hinting for weeks. And besides, I got this." He dug in his pocket and brought out a black velvet box. He snapped it open with two fingers.

Josie caught her breath. Nestled in the bed of satin was one of the prettiest diamond rings she'd ever seen. Big and round, and giving off colored light like a Fourth of July sparkler. Chase must pay his cutting trainers amazingly well…or else this guy had saved up for years.

"Wow," she said. "She's one lucky lady."

"Naw, I'm the lucky one," he said, flushing in the most endearing way. "She's flat-dab gorgeous, and I'm as ugly as homemade soap, but—"

He stopped midsentence, and stared at the door. "Well, I'll be damned." He frowned. "Excuse me, ma'am, but I was hoping I wouldn't have to lay eyes on that little gelding again so soon."

She looked at the door, too. And this time she did recognize the cowboy walking in. It was Eli Breslin, the kid Chase had fired last night. The boy glanced toward where she and Johnson stood, colored up, and then looked away, pretending he hadn't seen them.

"Good decision," Johnson grunted. "He better not push his luck. If it'd been up to me, he would've been fired from living, not just from that job. And I darn sure wouldn't have found work for him anywhere else."

He took a last swig of his sweet tea, then wiped his napkin across his mouth in one big sweep.

"But Mr. Clayton's got a soft heart, everybody knows that." He shrugged good-naturedly. "What can you do?"

"Mr. Clayton got Eli a new job already?"

"Yeah. At the hardware store. I guess it's okay, as long as he's not working with living critters. A person can't actually kill a monkey wrench, right?" He chuckled, amused at his own joke. "Though if anybody could, that's your boy."

The bushy-haired giant appeared suddenly from the kitchen, holding two huge white containers. "Two big muddies, ready to roll!"

Josie blinked, wondering where those

monster-sized boxes were going to fit in the van. And what was in them, anyhow? She leaned a little closer to Johnson and whispered, "What is a big muddy?"

He grinned. "Only the sweetest, gooiest, finger-lickin' fantastic chocolate cream pie this side of the Mississippi."

Josie sighed. Great. One more terrific, tempting thing that she couldn't allow herself to have. Not even if she used all the insulin this lovely new pump could produce.

She hesitated.

She'd said that the pie was one more tempting thing she couldn't have.

One more? That meant there had been another.

What was the other one?

But she didn't have to think very hard. She already knew the answer.

The other one was Chase.

CHAPTER TWELVE

CHASE WAS HOT, and tired and frustrated, and ready to call it a day. There were at least fifty people out here, helping to frame Drew Bradley's new house. Surely they could manage without him for the rest of the afternoon.

He wanted to get home and find out what the hell had happened between Trent and Susannah. Not that either one of them was likely to tell him the truth. They just might be the stubbornest two people on the planet. They kept everything inside.

Which was why, after eleven years, they still hadn't been able to work out their problems. And why they probably never would, not in a hundred more.

But just as he was about to track down

Liam, the framing contractor who'd come all the way from Madisonville to head up today's crew, and ask him to put someone else on measuring rafters, he saw Josie walking toward him. Her hands were full of red, yellow and white boxes.

Imogene's famous lunches. A roar of approval went up from the workers, most of whom had eaten Imogene's grub before. They gathered around Josie eagerly, and pretty soon a posse headed off to collect the rest of the boxes.

She stayed where she was, a red box in her hand, scanning the empty lot. She must have been looking for him, because when she spotted him, she smiled.

And suddenly he wasn't tired anymore.

He smiled back and crooked his hand to invite her over. He could have met her halfway, but he was enjoying the view too much. He watched her coming toward him, with that light sway in her hips, that natural bounce in her step.

He wondered what it was about her that always made him feel so…

Horny.

Sure, she was pretty, with that honey hair that swished around her shoulders, catching the afternoon sunlight. And those pink lips. And those subtle river-bottom-blue eyes fringed in feathery black lashes.

But what did he care about "pretty"? He'd dated true beauties. He'd been married to a woman who was off-the-charts gorgeous. Lila's lovers had written mournful ballads about her, and tragic Shakespearean sonnets. Rumor was that one of them had tried to kill himself. Another had applied to become a monk.

Maybe that was the difference, he thought. Lila made men miserable. Josie Whitford made them smile.

"Hi," she said as she finally reached him. "I bought you this, from Imogene. She put a dot here—" she pointed to the top right corner of the box "—so that I'd know exactly which one to give you. She didn't tell me why."

He laughed. "That's probably the one she put the poison in."

But when he opened it up, he saw what Imogene had planned. There were two sandwiches inside. One was ham, his usual. The other was a cucumber and egg salad sandwich—Josie's favorite. There was also a slice of chocolate cake, with a sticky note on the protective cellophane.

"Sugar free," the note read.

He wondered for a minute whether Imogene might be playing matchmaker, just a little. But his housekeeper idolized Susannah, so that didn't make any sense.

More likely, she'd grown fond of Josie, the same way everyone on his ranch had done. She probably thought it was unfair that Josie should just sit and drool while the rest of them gobbled up slices of Big Muddy.

"I think she hoped you'd stay and eat with me," he said. And he was absurdly pleased when Josie picked up the chocolate cake and grinned.

"You bet I will," she said. She kissed the cake. "Oh, Imogene, you are an angel!"

While she carried the box, he got them both big plastic cups of water. And then he led her over to the east side of the lot, the wooded side, where the property sloped off steeply toward Clayton Creek. Drew Bradley didn't have much—especially now that most of it had gone up in flames—but he did have one heavenly view down that daffodil-covered hillside.

They found a shady spot under a spreading maple, with the closest thing to privacy they were going to get today. At least fifteen feet and two trees lay between them and the other workers.

For several minutes they ate in silence. Imogene's food was too good to give it only half your attention. They'd grown comfortable with each other, he realized. Sometime in the past ten days, they'd relaxed enough to be silent together. It was a good place— one he'd never reached with Lila.

Finally, their appetites were satisfied. Josie put her napkin and empty cup inside the box, then stretched out along the grass, tilting her head back so that her face could catch the dappled sunlight through the leaves.

He scanned her body, assessing her condition. She wore shorts and a T-shirt, which gave him a good view from head to toe. He could even see the tiniest swell at her abdomen, which might have been the first outward sign of the baby.

It made the baby real, as nothing else had done so far, not even the visit to Dunne. It was growing there, inside her. Some man had created this life with her, and had walked away from it.

The bloody fool should be taken out back and shot.

She was still dramatically slender, but finally it looked healthy, the slightly bony, long-legged look of a new foal. Strong. Full of life. She looked as if she could run down this hill, the wind in her hair and the daffodils at her feet, and splash into the creek at the bottom, laughing and panting.

He had a sudden ache, wanting to see her do that. Wanting to do it with her. He'd like to lift her up onto Captain Kirk's broad, slow-moving back and ride her under the trees. He'd take her to Green

Fern Hole and show her the two-winged silverbell.

But if he did that…how exactly was he any different from the bastard who had gotten her pregnant in the first place? Was a condom really all that stood between right and wrong?

He wadded his napkin up hard in his hand and squeezed it till his joints turned white.

"You awake?" Her voice was soft, as if she didn't want to disturb him, in case he'd dozed off.

"Yeah," he said. He tried to remove the tension from his tone. She wouldn't have any idea what had caused it. Her thoughts undoubtedly weren't turgid, as obsessed with sex as a teenager.

"I just wanted to tell you. When I stopped by the diner to get the pie, I looked at all the pictures they have in there. I thought maybe, if Flim lived here at any time, he might have been photographed at one of the events."

"Not a bad idea. And?"

She shook her head. "Nothing. I didn't recognize anyone."

"Don't worry. We'll find him sooner or later. I'm thinking about sending a private investigator to Riverfork. Maybe Flim did something dumb, like pay for a hotel or a meal with his own credit card. He's mortal, right? He has to have made a misstep somewhere."

She looked at him a minute. Then she sat up, cross-legged, with her hands in her lap. Her face was solemn. "How long do you intend to keep hunting, Chase?"

"Until we find him."

"But what if we don't? What if there is no logic we can apply, no description we can come up with, that will tie him to you? What if he's just some random guy, some person you've never even met? He could have heard the stories about you thirdhand. You're sort of a celebrity around here. People talk about you. Stories get passed around."

"I don't believe that," he said. "My gut tells me I know this guy. I just have to find out how, and where."

"And what if it takes a long time? What if it takes months?"

He shrugged. "Fine."

"What if it takes years? Do you want me to be hanging around your guest room when the baby is starting school? Would it still be fine then?"

"Sure. Why not? The schools around here are great."

She plucked a blade of grass absently. She gazed into the mid-distance, still smiling, but with a faraway look that held a touch of sadness.

Finally she looked back at him. "I think it's time for me to go."

"Why?" He frowned, suddenly irritable. "You said yourself there's nothing for you to go back to. If you're bored, take a class or something. If you want a job, I've got plenty of them here on the ranch."

"No. You've been more than generous. But I can't go on being your charity case."

He felt heat tighten the muscles of his chest. That "charity" line just didn't wash anymore. They had become friends, and he would do as much for any friend. Besides, she worked so hard around the house she ought to be getting a salary.

And it just plain didn't ring true. She wasn't being completely honest with him, and he had a feeling he knew why.

"Look, Josie. If this is about last night…"

"It isn't," she said, too quickly. The flush on her face wasn't merely from the sun. "I know that didn't mean anything. It was just…just the river and the moonlight. And you feeling sorry for me because I was feeling a little—"

"No," he said, making a conscious effort to keep his voice low. Their neighbors were close enough to hear everything if they weren't careful. "It had nothing to do with pity. It was just what it seemed to be. Me wanting to kiss you so much I thought I'd go crazy."

Her eyes widened. "Chase—"

"But I know it was a mistake. It was the dumbest thing I could possibly have done, for more reasons than I can possibly count. You don't have to worry, and you damn sure don't have to run away. I won't do it again."

"I know," she said. "And honestly, that's not why I'm thinking of leaving. It was no big deal, in the end. It was just a kiss."

Not even that, he wanted to say. It had been only half a kiss. Only the tiniest fraction of what he'd wanted to do. Of what he could make her feel.

If he were free… If she were free…

But they weren't.

"The truth is…I need to start making some decisions about my future." She touched her stomach with the palms of her hands. "September will be here so soon, and I'm not ready."

"No one is telling you not to make plans. Just make them here, where you've got a support system—good doctors, good food. A comfortable roof over your head."

He couldn't believe he was doing this. He was getting married in a month. He had no right to get emotionally involved with this woman. He'd talked to Susannah about it, and had admitted that, though at first he'd been involved only so that he could find the impostor, it had morphed into something else. Josie's vulnerability moved him. He felt oddly guilty, because the creep who left her like this had used his name.

He knew it didn't make sense, but he wanted to help her. To provide at least a little piece of the safety net she needed.

As usual, Sue had been a brick. She'd made a joke about his superhero syndrome. And then she'd assured him that she had no problem with any decision he made. He could help Josie in any way that seemed fair.

So, officially, he had his fiancée's blessing.

But, deep inside, he knew he wasn't telling Susannah everything. When he was with Josie, he wasn't just a protective uncle, or a friendly pal, or a fairy godfather.

He was a man. And she was a woman.

Whether he allowed himself to act on it or not, it was disloyal to Sue, to whom he had already promised his support.

Now that Josie had said she wanted to go home, he should wish her Godspeed. In spite of what Susannah said, he didn't think he was a superhero. He couldn't make everything right for everyone.

When she went back to Riverfork, he could stay in touch. He could send money to help with the baby. He could arrange for good prenatal care.

Why wasn't that enough?

Was it possible that, in less than two weeks, he had grown so accustomed to her presence in his house that he couldn't imagine the place without her?

Next thing he knew he'd be offering her a job as his housekeeper. Or his secretary.

Or his mistress.

"Stay through the weekend, anyhow," he suggested, grasping at straws. "Come with me to the horse auction on Sunday. A lot of the people I've done business with through the years will be there. If nothing comes of all that, I'll take you home on Monday."

She bit her lower lip. She was obviously deeply conflicted. He was sorry for that. But not sorry enough to make her decision any easier.

"I did tell Susannah I'd come to the

Burn Center's dance tomorrow night. Not that I can afford to make any kind of donation, but—"

"She didn't ask you because she wanted a donation. She asked you because she thought you might enjoy it."

She took a deep breath. "All right. I'll stay through the weekend. But then, if we haven't found him—"

"I know," he said. "If we haven't found him, I promise I'll take you home."

AT SEVEN O'CLOCK Saturday night, just two hours before the fund-raiser dance would begin, Susannah stood in her bathroom and prayed for courage.

"Okay. Here goes." She wrapped a hank of hair around the curling iron, wound it tightly and held it for the count of ten. The thick coat of styling gel began to heat up, and she wrinkled her nose against the nasty, fruity scent.

God, why did anybody *do* this? When she unrolled her curl, her hair looked fake and shiny, like a lardy sausage. But she refused to be daunted. She picked up another section of hair and began the process all over again.

This was the last step. She'd already completed her makeup, and she was quite pleased with the results. She smiled at herself in the mirror, trying to get used to seeing big black feathers of mascara whenever she blinked. She licked her juicy red lips, showing a lot of pink tongue.

Perfect. She looked like the love child of Marilyn Manson and Cleopatra. She positively oozed sex. And not good-girl sex, either. Hot, trashy, male-fantasy sex.

The kind of sex she'd never had in her life.

Her clothes had been the toughest part. Nothing she owned was even close. Her closet was full of tailored slacks and blazers, and cool, expensive evening dresses that all shivered icily and said *don't touch me, I'm channeling Jacqueline Kennedy*.

So she'd spent the afternoon in Austin, trying on the most seductive clubbing outfits she could find. Some of them had made her blush, even in the privacy of the dressing room. The white bell-bottoms, for instance, that had the rear end cut out and a built-in white thong to cover the indecency laws. Or the skintight black dress with pink sequin nipples appliquéd on the chest.

Okay, maybe the situation with Nicole wasn't as bad as it could possibly get. Compared to these outfits, Nikki's clothes looked like Pollyanna pinafores.

She settled on an all-white minidress and a pair of thigh-high black boots. The dress was too tight, too short—and just trashy enough to make her point without getting her arrested.

She squinted her eyes as she finished the last curl, and smiled a smug-cat smile. She couldn't wait to see Nikki's face.

She had to hurry, though. The whole purpose would be defeated if she didn't get down there before Nikki chose her own outfit.

She heard Nikki trudging up the stairs, every heavy footfall announcing how much she didn't want to attend tonight's dance. Two days ago, she'd been thrilled.

But the difference was that, two days ago, Eli had been invited.

Nikki had only one way of making Susannah pay. By dressing like a trashy little hoodlum, she could advertise her disdain for Susannah's stodgy, middle-class attitude toward work and life, toward love and money. Plus, she could embarrass Susannah in front of her equally self-righteous friends at the Burn Center.

The minidress was Susannah's somewhat dramatic plan to stage a preemptive strike.

When she heard Nikki hit the landing, she stepped out of the bathroom, zipping up her last boot. She tugged her microscopic skirt over her rear end, and smiled at her little sister. "Hey, Nik. Is my slip showing?"

Oh, for the foresight to have brought along her Polaroid! Nikki's expression was priceless. She had been scratching an itch in the center of her back, and she froze that way, her elbow pointing toward the ceiling. Her mouth fell open, giving Susannah a clear look at her tonsils.

She seemed, for a minute, incapable of speech. That alone had to be counted as a victory.

"Oh, that's right! Silly me! I'm not wearing a slip." Susannah twisted her hip and pretended to be looking at her own butt. "But what do you think about underwear? Yes or no? I don't want to have a panty line, but…"

Finally Nikki lowered her arm. "What the *hell* are you thinking?"

"Don't cuss, sweetie. And you'd better hurry. We've got to leave in about twenty minutes."

Nikki's eyebrows dug so deep over her eyes Susannah wondered how she could see. "What is this? Some kind of joke?"

"No, of course not. I just listened to what you said yesterday, you know, about how I've forgotten how to have fun. You're right. I need to loosen up a little bit." She plumped her crazy curls. "I thought I'd start tonight."

"Are you out of your mind?"

"Of course not," she said again, quite

merrily. "I'm just letting go of my inhibitions."

She picked up her atomizer and began spraying perfume. One puff. Two. Three. She could hardly breathe, but she managed to squeeze out a fourth. She held back a cough and extended the atomizer to Nikki. "Want some?"

Nikki backed up. "No," she said adamantly. "You smell like a toxic waste dump. You're going to suffocate everybody in the place."

Susannah sighed. "Don't be so uptight, Nikki." She turned back to the bathroom and rummaged in her jewelry case. She lifted out the rhinestone chandelier dangles she'd bought at the boutique today. They weighed about five pounds each. "What do you think? I don't think it's too much, do you?"

"I think you'll look like a slut. You already do look like one."

Nikki folded her arms over her chest. She seemed a bit unnerved, and for a minute Susannah had a pang of conscience. Had she gone too far? Might

Nikki really be afraid that her only guardian had lost her mind?

"Sue," she said. "Get real. I'm not going anywhere with you dressed like that."

"Of course you are. You're giving a speech, remember? About the children's wing?"

"Then you have to take off that outfit. And the makeup, too. You look awful."

"What do you care what I wear?" She raised her eyebrows. "Are you implying that it would embarrass you to be seen with me?"

Nikki started to answer, but she slammed her mouth shut. Her expression changed, moving from bewildered to darkly sullen.

"Oh, I get it," she said slowly. "You're trying to make a point. But I'm not that stupid, you know. God, what a lame-ass trick."

"Trick?"

"Yeah, trick. You want me to admit that this is what I do to you, when I wear clothes you don't like. But it's not the same."

"It isn't?" Susannah put one booted foot

up on the vanity stool, bent over and ran her hands across the formfitting plastic. "How exactly is it different?"

Nikki hesitated. Her debating skills weren't all that well honed yet. But she did her best. "Well, you're a lot older than I am, for one thing."

Susannah widened her bloodred lips. "I'm thirty. And I think I look pretty darn good in these boots, if I do say so myself."

"Chase will hate it. He'll be really mad."

"Oh, I doubt that." Susannah turned to the mirror so that she could insert one of the dangles into her ear. "But even if he is, why should that bother you? He's not *your* boyfriend."

Nikki didn't have an answer for that one, which made her angrier than ever. In the mirror, Susannah could see that she was holding on to the banister knob. Her fingertips were bloodless white.

"It's not going to work, you know," Nikki said. "I'm still going to wear whatever I want."

"Good!" Susannah forced delight into

her voice as she slid in the other dangle. "We can be like twins. The Slutty Everly Sisters. It'll be fun."

Nikki sputtered something, then gave up and stomped away.

As Susannah heard the violent sound of the bedroom door slamming shut, she turned around slowly. Sighing, she hoisted her barely covered rump onto the countertop and stared down at her trashy plastic boots.

Okay, so… She'd seriously miscalculated. Her sister was way too savvy, and the whole charade had somehow turned into a do-or-die game of chicken.

Well, she darn sure wasn't going to blink first.

Which meant it was going to be a very interesting evening. She tried to picture herself giving the "please give generously to our worthy cause" speech in these boots.

And this microskirt would give a whole new meaning to the electric slide.

She kicked the cabinet with her heels. But hey, why not look on the bright side?

At least she could count on some great big, drooling donations from the dirty old men in the room.

CHAPTER THIRTEEN

JOSIE LOVED TO DANCE.

Riverfork didn't have much going for it, but every Saturday night the Barbecue Barn rolled up the tables and held a "Stomping Good Barn Dance" that actually lived up to its name. The Taylors, who owned the restaurant, were her friends, and Josie never missed a week if she could help it.

So when Susannah invited her to the Burn Center's barn dance fund-raiser, she had accepted eagerly. This was one place where she could definitely hold her own.

Especially tonight, when, for the first time in a long time she felt good, and she knew she looked good. She had on a new pair of jeans that she'd bought in town the other day, when she and Chase had gone to visit the sketch artist. She even had a new shirt—a turquoise-blue sleeveless tank top with a fairly daring V-neck. It had taken the very last penny she owned that wasn't needed to pay the bills, but it was worth it. Both pieces fit just right, especially now that Imogene's food had put a few pounds back where they belonged.

Best of all, though, was the special decoration she wore in her hair. She'd been almost finished dressing, when Chase knocked on the guest room door. *Wow*, she thought instinctively…with those tight hips and sexy rear end, he was like a walking advertisement for blue jeans. And when he topped it off with that soft-as-baby-skin white shirt and crisp navy blazer, he was really something special.

"I thought you might like to wear this," he said.

She pulled her thoughts together. In his outstretched hand, he held an exquisite little hair clip.

"It belonged to my mother," he said. "I know she'd like you to have it."

When she hesitated, he assured her it wasn't an expensive piece, though she found that hard to believe. Handmade, it was an intricate spiderweb of fine silver, studded with blue topaz. And from the spiderweb hung several small, shining peacock feathers.

A dream catcher.

That was what won her over. Everyone in Texas knew the legend of the dream catcher—the hole in the center of the spiderweb let the good dreams come through, while the web itself trapped and destroyed the nightmares. The dangling feathers helped to guide wisdom and comfort to the sleeper.

How could she resist? Who didn't need some help catching and holding on to the right dreams?

So she had accepted. She pulled the hair back from the sides of her face, and clipped it all into the silver band. Delighted, she had swiveled, trying to see it in the mirror, and every time she moved the feathers swung, tickling against her ear and neck.

It made her feel very special. Very feminine. Almost beautiful.

That cocky glow lasted about twenty minutes. Right up until the instant they arrived at the big, elaborately decorated Thompson Ranch barn, the donated site for the dance.

Right up until the minute she saw Susannah Everly.

This fund-raiser was Susannah's event, Chase had explained. The Burn Center was her special project, and she'd been planning the dance for months.

So, to prepare, Susannah had arrived long before everyone else. She stood on stage talking to the banjo player, with several other musicians hovering on her every word.

She looked unbelievable.

Josie had assumed that this dance would be much like the ones in Riverfork, casual and folksy, with lots of beer and laughter. Denim and flannel everywhere.

Obviously she'd made a mistake. Susannah looked as if she'd just finished a cover shoot for Vogue magazine. She wore the sexiest little white dress Josie had ever seen, and thigh-high boots that proved beyond a shadow of a doubt that she had the longest, sexiest legs in Texas. She'd topped the whole daring outfit off with a small white cowboy hat trimmed with a wide jade ribbon as green as her eyes.

When they saw her, Josie stopped dead in her tracks. But Chase laughed, then let out a loud, salacious wolf whistle.

"Lawsie Miss Suzie," he said, laughing as he moved in and kissed his fiancée on the cheek. "You are one hot number tonight."

To Josie's surprise, Susannah grimaced. "Not by choice," she said cryptically. "Suffice it to say…I have finally learned what it truly means to be hoist by one's own petard."

Chase cocked his head. "Huh?"

"Tell you later. It's a long story, and frankly it makes me look like an idiot." Belatedly, Susannah noticed Josie. "Hey, there," she said with a smile. "I'm glad you felt up to coming."

"I couldn't wait," Josie said honestly. She'd been edgy and excited all day, whenever she thought about it. "You look terrific. But I have to admit I'm suddenly feeling a bit underdressed."

"You look just right," Susannah assured her. "Believe me, if anyone is under-dressed, it's me."

"You're right about that, honey." Chase laughed. "Not that I'm complaining, but… you sure you didn't leave the bottom half of that dress at home in the box?"

Susannah gave him a dark look. "Very funny. Now I'd better get back to business here. I've got to open this party." She touched Chase's arm. "Why don't you and Josie check out the buffet? I'll see you later, okay?"

After that, things were a bit of a blur. Everyone, it seemed, wanted to meet Josie. She could guess, from the curious glances and the eager questions, that her dramatic arrival at Clayton Creek Ranch had been the hot gossip for days. What was this mystery woman? Friend? Lover? A little of both?

Chase handled it smoothly, introducing her over and over as Josie Whitford, his good friend from Riverfork. He was quite convincing, telling in sympathetic detail the harrowing story of her long drive, her eagerness to arrive in time for the party, the low blood sugar and the crash.

He was so plausible that even the people who looked the most skeptical at the outset went away persuaded that he'd known her forever, almost like brother and sister.

By the time he was through, Josie half believed it herself.

For a full half hour, while Susannah stood on stage with a microphone, discussing the Burn Center and introducing the guests of honor, including the callers and the musicians, Chase devoted himself to Josie.

He was a charming date, careful to keep the conversation general enough to include her, and attentive to her every need. He brought her a sparkling water with a twist of lime, and then found her a plateful of salad and grilled chicken. He led her to a table where they could sit with Trent and some of the others from the ranch.

But the truth nagged at her. He wasn't her date—he was Susannah's, and pretty soon the other woman would be free of her official duties, and she'd come looking for her man.

Josie hated knowing that he probably felt trapped. She hated being the social albatross around his neck.

So when a tall, brown-haired cowboy in a rawhide vest came up and asked her to dance, she accepted.

Chase, who had just been approached by a couple of middle-aged ladies, didn't seem to mind. He smiled and lifted a hand to signify his approval.

It was an easy line dance, and her partner moved well, so Josie had a ball. She hadn't danced since before Chase...before *Flim* walked through the doors of the Not Guilty Café and turned her life upside down.

In a way, this dance felt like an official reentry into real life.

Her cowboy—whose name was Hallem— asked for the next dance, too—another line dance, which must be the way they'd decided to warm up the crowd. She said yes again.

They were on their third, the first slow song of the night, when Chase appeared and tapped on Hallem's shoulder.

"Sorry, Hal," he said good-naturedly. "You can't monopolize her all night."

"Oh, well. It was worth a try," the cowboy said. He bowed with a flourish, kissed Josie's hand and slowly sauntered away.

"You don't mind, do you?" Chase smiled. "You're supposed to dance at least one dance with the guy who brought you."

No, she didn't mind. Josie hadn't really dared to hope that he would be willing to ask her. He'd gone to so much trouble to convince everyone that they were just good friends. Of course, good friends danced together all the time. Maybe it would seem more suspicious if they didn't.

The truth was that, where he was concerned, she'd completely lost her bearings. She no longer knew what was normal and what wasn't. Sometimes she felt absolutely sure they were friends, real friends, even though they'd known each other such a short time.

Sometimes that seemed like the silliest kind of wishful thinking.

She looked at him, his thick golden hair catching the light from the antler candelabra that had been jury-rigged especially for this occasion. When she met his gaze, her entire body seemed to tighten and shimmer, and surely that meant something.

But what?

Maybe it was gratitude. Or hormones. Or transference.

Maybe it was just the same bone-deep loneliness that had made her open her door, her bed and her heart to the last guy who had been flattering and kind.

She no longer trusted her own feelings. How could she? She had made such a terrible mistake the last time she…

She held her breath, realizing what she had been about to say to herself.

She'd made such a terrible mistake the last time she fell in love with Chase Clayton.

She glanced around, feeling panicked.

The feathers of her dream catcher fluttered at her ear.

"Hey." His voice was soft. He held out his arms. "It's okay, Josie. Just dance with me."

He might as well have hypnotized her. Even while she was telling her mouth to say no, her legs were moving toward him. She put her hand on his shoulder. He wrapped his fingers around her other hand, and closed it in against his chest.

There was nothing inappropriate about their posture. She kept her eyes open, and didn't let her head tilt even an inch toward his body. He didn't let his hand slip to the sensitive small of her back, or press her in too close.

From the outside, they probably looked like any other couple in the room.

But from the inside, it was pure dynamite. Tiny gold and white fireworks were popping inside her veins. His hand was so hot she felt sure that tonight, when she took off her shirt, she'd find his brand on her spine. Under her fingers, his heart was pumping hard and slow, in a bolero rhythm that made her think of sex.

Deep in her body, the same rhythm answered. A fist of desire squeezed rhythmically, opening and shutting, creating ebbs and flows of heat, until she wasn't sure she could breathe.

She shivered. In a minute, in a second, in one more dangerous heartbeat, her eyes would drift shut. Her body would soften. Her skin would begin to glow.

And everyone would see.

But the song was already ending. As the last notes of the violin reverberated under the high ceilings, and the dancers began to clap, she pulled away.

She looked at him, oddly dazed. Hardly seeing him.

"I need to—" She frowned, and looked toward the exit. "I should…the—"

His hand touched her back again. "Are you all right? Do you feel unwell?"

"No, Chase," she said. She took a deep breath. "I feel confused."

He might have been about to answer

her, but she didn't get the chance to find out. Trent was suddenly at his shoulder, tapping it.

"My turn, corporal," he said with a wry smile. "And unless I miss my guess, there's a hot dominatrix cowgirl over there who's wondering where you are."

Chase glanced toward their table, where Susannah had just settled with a glass of wine in one hand, and a horse-whip in the other.

He laughed. "Who can resist an invitation like that?"

He looked down at Josie, and his gaze was as neutral and friendly as if none of the fireworks had ever happened.

"Thanks for the dance," he said. "Have fun with Trent, and try not to let him break all your toes at once."

Trent made an irritated noise, swept Josie into his arms and swung her into a graceful waltzing rhythm.

His arms were strong and sure. He was a superb dancer, and just as handsome as Chase. Maybe, technically, even more so.

And yet...no fireworks. Not even the tiniest spark.

"So," he began pleasantly. "Are you having a good time?"

She nodded. "I haven't danced in ages. It feels great."

"I was watching you with Chase," he said. "You're a good dancer. Of course, anyone looks good when they're standing next to his two left feet."

She smiled, not bothering to contradict him, even though he couldn't be more wrong. Chase was such a natural that it didn't even feel like dancing—it just felt like fusing bodies and moving as one.

Obviously neither man meant his insults to be taken seriously. They were just two Alpha dogs playing, teeth bared, but no real damage done. They were the two best-looking, most charismatic men here tonight—and that was quite a statement, given that this huge barn was now filled with healthy, studly sun-kissed cowboys dressed to kill.

Yet, every time they danced in Chase's

direction, she couldn't help watching him. He sat next to Susannah. His arm was draped casually across the back of her chair, and they were head-to-head, whispering over their drinks.

After a couple of turns, she caught Trent looking at her, that wry, one-sided smile on his lips.

"They look good together, don't they?"

She nodded, trying not to blush. "Susannah is amazing. I can't imagine having the courage to wear that dress. And yet she looks fantastic."

"It's definitely not her usual style," he said, his eyes studying the brunette beauty as they went by. "She's ordinarily pretty straitlaced. You know what they're saying, don't you?"

"What who is saying?"

"Everyone." He leaned his head back, so that he could get a straight look at her. "They're saying that Sue had to ramp up the sex appeal tonight, because she was afraid she was losing her man."

Josie stumbled, nearly stepping on Trent's toes. *"What?"*

He nodded, still watching her closely. "Yeah, crazy, huh? But I actually heard someone say it, straight to her face."

"But that's absurd—"

"Well," he said conversationally, "you and I know it's absurd. And we certainly hope that Chase knows it, too. But I'm not so sure what Sue knows."

Josie couldn't figure out exactly what Trent's interest was in all this. It was as if someone had appointed him guardian of Susannah's love life, although, from a few of Chase's indirect comments, Josie had gathered that Trent and Susannah didn't much like each other.

"I'm not sure whether I'm reading between the lines correctly here. But if you, or anyone, think I'm getting into some kind of competition with Susannah, you couldn't be more wrong. Do I find Chase attractive? Of course I do. Poll the females in this room, and find me even one who doesn't."

Trent chuckled. "Yeah. I guess that proves women are nuts."

She looked him straight in the eye. "But

I know this marriage is very important to her. I wouldn't interfere with that, even if I could. And I couldn't."

He raised one eyebrow. "What makes you think you couldn't?"

"Come on, Trent." She smiled. "Pretend it's a horse race, and look at the tip sheets on each of us. Based on history, bloodline, experience, conditioning, familiarity with the track... She wins by a mile, in any weather, on any surface."

"Maybe so—on paper, anyhow. Sounds as if you're a gambler."

"No. But my stepfather was."

"Then you also know what a dark horse is. A long shot. And you know that they've been known to come in. Especially if the horse is ready, and she wants it bad enough."

She was suddenly weary of the racing metaphor.

She didn't want to spend this whole party trying to read between the lines of the complicated Clayton social set. She hadn't been to a party in months, and she wanted to enjoy herself.

"Don't worry, Trent," she said. "This is one dark horse that isn't coming in anywhere except on the scratch sheet."

"The scratch sheet?"

"Yes. You can tell Susannah she's got nothing to worry about. When Monday comes, I'm going home."

CHAPTER FOURTEEN

THEY LAUGHED AND SANG all the way home, as if they were drunk, even though neither one of them had touched liquor all night. Josie had the baby to consider, and Chase... well, he hadn't had a drink for ten years, not since the night of Paul's accident.

He loved to see her so happy, especially after the tension of their dance. Somehow she'd seemed to shrug it off, and she'd wholeheartedly thrown herself into having fun.

Maybe she realized that, if she was going back home on Monday, this might be her last chance to feel so free, to dance and laugh and set aside all thoughts of the future.

He wanted her to make the most of it. So he'd fed the happiness everything he could find, trying to prolong it. He brought her delicious food and exotic virgin cocktails. He'd introduced her to all the most entertaining people, and he'd asked the band to play the songs he knew she'd liked.

But the real hilarity had started when she finally won a door prize. The really great stuff at the dance was all up for auction—it was a fund-raiser, after all. Obviously Josie couldn't bid on any of that, but there were several door prizes, too, and she'd set her heart on winning one of them.

She'd held her breath while they gave away the weekend in Galveston. She'd said a prayer when the turquoise earrings were up. She'd even crossed her fingers, hoping to be called for the Swedish massage.

But she hadn't won any of those. Instead, when they hollered out her ticket number, it was for a big, hulking black saddle.

A buffalo buckstitched pleasure saddle, to be exact.

Wouldn't you just know it? The expression on her face was priceless. She'd climbed the stage, trying to look thrilled, but when they handed her the saddle it was clear she didn't even know how to hold it—much less how to use it.

"I'm sorry," she said now, still smiling as they approached the front door of the Double C. "I know in your world saddles are serious business. It's just that—"

She started to giggle again. "Why do they call it—"

He tried to get the key in the lock. But it wasn't easy when you were laughing. "A pleasure saddle?"

Her eyes danced. "And not just any pleasure saddle. A buffalo buttstitched...I mean...a buffalo suttbicked..."

She simply couldn't say it. Laughter had tied a knot in her tongue. She put her hand over her mouth. "Oh, lord. I'm going to wake up Imogene."

"She's not here, remember? She's with her sister in Austin. Laugh as loud as you want. You might annoy the horses, but there's no one else to complain."

She inhaled deeply, hiccupping mid-breath, which set off another round of giggles. She leaned against the siding, trying to get control.

He smiled. He knew this was his fault. All the way home, he'd done everything but stand on his head to amuse her, egging her on, making it worse, hoping she wouldn't ever stop.

He loved the sound of her giggles. He basked in the glow on her face.

He wasn't the only one. He'd seen it all night long, on the faces of the other men. She was so full of life—she seemed essential, like the bubble in your champagne.

Every man at the party between seven and seventy had wanted to dance with her, and most of them had.

It hadn't been easy, standing back while they spun her on the floor, twirled her and do-si-doed her, linked hands with her to shoot the star. She had a natural grace, and a wellspring of enthusiasm that acted like a magnet, pulling other people to her, so that they could share in the joy.

It was all he could do to keep from cutting in every couple of dances. He held back by reminding himself that maybe these guys could hold her hand…but he was the lucky cowboy who would get to take her home.

And Imogene wasn't there.

Finally he got the lock open. He held the door wide, stepped aside and let her through. She danced into the foyer, then twirled her way into the library, where she dropped with a sigh onto the sofa.

He followed, the ridiculous saddle draped over his left arm.

"Oh, my goodness," she said, sighing as she kicked off her shoes. "You must think I'm such a dork."

"Must I?' He arranged the saddle carefully over the arm of the sofa, spreading out the fenders so that they dangled free. "Why?"

She grinned up at him. "Because I'm pretty sure only twelve-year-old boys think words are funny just because they rhyme with buck."

He chuckled.

"A sophomoric sense of humor isn't your

biggest sin," he said. He made a small adjustment on the saddle, so that it balanced more securely. "The real shame is that you don't appreciate what a nice door prize you just won. Any guy at the party would gladly have bought it from you."

"No way." She leaned across and placed a protective hand over the black leather seat. "This beauty is mine."

"Oh, yeah? What do you plan to do with it?"

"I'm going to use it," she said. She wrinkled her cute nose. "As soon as I learn how."

"Okay. How about if I teach you?"

She cocked her head, giving him a quizzical look. "Now?"

"Yeah. Right now. Come on, tenderfoot. Let's see how you do."

He reached down, grabbed her hands and lifted her to a standing position.

She protested laughingly, but didn't pull away. Obediently, she let him arrange her on the far side of the couch.

"Let's start with the mount," he said.

"Face me, grab hold of the horn, then throw your right leg over the saddle."

She did as she was told, smiling at the foolishness of it. The leather creaked gently under her weight, but it didn't slip. As soon as she was situated, she gripped the sofa with her knees.

She wriggled her bottom on the leather seat, finding the most comfortable spot.

"No problem." She gripped the horn with both hands. "See? I'm a natural."

"Not so fast, there, Annie Oakley." He pried her fingers free. "You can't hold on to the horn while you're riding. You'll need your hands for the reins. That's how you'll tell the horse what you want him to do."

She raised her brows. "I want him to go very, very slowly and never toss me off."

"No, you don't. That would be much too boring." He held out his arms. "Here. Put your hands here. I'll be your reins."

She glanced up at him, hesitating slightly, her eyes darkened just enough to tell him that their lighthearted foolishness might be turning into something else.

But then, with a nervous smile, she wrapped her fingers around his wrists. They felt warm and slightly tremulous against his skin.

"Good." He squared off his feet, bracing his knees against the sofa. "Now, remember—riding won't always be as easy as this. For one thing, the horse will be moving under you."

Without warning, he pulled back his arms slightly, causing her to rock forward. She gasped, and balanced herself again.

"See? Not so simple. If you're going to stay on, you have to learn to move with him."

He tugged again, and this time she was ready. She leaned toward him, tucking her seat forward, lifting just a little with her knees.

"That's right. Just like that." He moved her yet again. "Forward, then back. Forward, then back."

She rocked in place slowly, tilting her pelvis toward the horn when he told her to, letting him control the rhythm.

"Chase," she began. But she didn't say

anything else. She seemed to need all her focus to keep her balance.

He held her gaze with his. "Good," he said. "Nice and steady. Just let it flow."

She swallowed hard, nodding. He never increased the rhythm, but after a minute or two her fingers tightened against his wrists, and her breath started to come faster.

He knew what was happening to her. He also knew he ought to stop.

But he was shameless—and he couldn't even offer the excuse that he'd been carried away by the moment. On some subconscious level, at least, this was premeditated, and he knew it.

Ever since they had danced together, he'd been thinking of something like this, of finding an excuse to touch her, to take the heat that simmered between them and bring it to the boiling point.

He knew it would be this easy. Her senses had already been spiking, tonight, when they were dancing. In fact, for the past several days, every time they were together, they both rode dangerously close to the edge.

"Don't stop," she said softly. He looked down and realized that his arms had frozen in place.

"Josie, we should—"

"No, please." She shut her eyes. "Please, Chase. It feels so good."

He couldn't say no. He was already too far gone. He began again, and she let her head fall back with a low moan. The dream catcher feathers dangled free, swaying to the same steady, unrelenting beat.

She was so unguarded, and so beautiful. He felt himself hardening, caught up in the rhythm, too, helplessly turned on by the sight of her flushed cheeks, her parted lips. By the feel of her fingers, tightening, trembling, holding on to his wrists as if they were the only steady spot in a tilting universe.

"Josie," he whispered.

She opened her eyes. They were unfocused, shining and bemused.

He bent his arms slowly, bringing them up toward his chest. She didn't let go. She followed them, bending her torso over the horn, making a soft noise as she pressed hard against the leather.

At the moment their lips met, she whispered his name.

That was all he needed. He freed his arms, and wrapped them around her, lifting her from the saddle.

She wound her legs around his hips, meeting his fire with her own. This wasn't a game anymore. It wasn't just a clever seduction with props and toys.

If there had been any seduction tonight, it was she who seduced him.

He didn't want her to find her release there, against the stiff leather of the horn. He wanted her in his arms, with her mouth against his, so that when she cried out he could feel it reverberate all the way through him.

He kissed her hard, with every ounce of heat and conviction he'd held back the last time. He wound his hands into her hair, his fingers catching on feathers. He throbbed painfully against his jeans, as desperate as a teenager, needing to be in her now, before it was too late.

He carried her to the sofa, and they fell together against the cool, slick leather. She was still rocking under him, fumbling with his buckle. Somehow he managed her zipper, and began to slide the jeans down her silken thighs.

And then the doorbell rang.

SUSANNAH HATED to bother Chase so late at night, especially after he'd been such a sweetheart at the party, square-dancing with old ladies who had big bank accounts and talking bloodlines with the old guys who had fat checkbooks, just to help the Burn Center.

Thanks, in part, to his special, home-spun charm, the dance had been a financial success.

But the rest of her evening had been a complete disaster.

And frankly, she needed a friend.

No one came to the door. She wondered if he'd already gone to bed. Ordinarily he stayed up a while, reading in the library, but maybe he didn't do that anymore, now that he had a guest in the house.

She rang again. Maybe he was on the back porch.

The door jerked open quite suddenly. It was Chase, and thank goodness he didn't look annoyed at being disturbed in the middle of the night.

"Hey, there," he said with a smile. "You're up late. Is everything okay?"

"No," she said. "Not really. Would it be okay if I come in? I think I just need someone to talk to."

"Sure," he said. He stepped away from the door. "Josie's heading to bed, but I'm not quite ready to turn in."

She looked over his shoulder and saw Josie on the first landing. The young woman looked uncomfortable, and oddly tousled.

"Hi," Josie said, holding on to the banister with one stiff hand. She smiled, but the smile didn't look right, either. Her lips seemed swollen. Susannah wondered whether she might have been crying. "The dance was fantastic, Susannah. I hope you made a ton of money for the Burn Center."

"We did very well," Susannah said, trying to identify the odd nuances of this situation. "I'm glad you could come."

If she didn't know better, she might think that she'd interrupted something awkward. The problem was, she was so unsettled by her own bad news that she couldn't really focus on anything else.

"Me, too." Josie smiled again. She lifted her hand in a stiff wave. "Well, good night, then."

"Good night," Chase said politely. Then, as Josie disappeared around the turn in the stairs, he gestured toward the library. "Want to talk in here?"

Susannah followed him in, less comfortable than she could ever remember feeling in Chase's house. Something definitely wasn't right.

"Have you and Josie been quarreling?"

Chase glanced at her over his shoulder. "Of course not. She just tires easily. It's the pregnancy, I guess."

Susannah nodded. "I guess so."

It sounded plausible, but…

She'd known Chase so long, it was hard for him to hide anything from her. She knew all his expressions, all his tones. She knew what he looked like when he was lying about something minor, like telling her a haircut looked good when it didn't, or telling his dad he'd missed curfew because he'd run out of gas.

She also knew what he looked like when he was lying about something important, like when he'd tried to tell her his marriage was doing fine. Or when he told her he really believed Paul was going to be all right.

This was something in between. Not a major whopper, but not a tiny white one, either.

"Want something to drink?" Chase made his way to the big granite bar over near the fireplace. "I've got some wine, some beer…"

"No, thanks," she said. She went straight to the sofa and plopped down, so glad to get off her feet, which were killing her from hours of standing in those boots. The first thing she'd done when she got home was whip off the whole ridiculous outfit and put on a pair of jeans and sneakers instead.

The second thing she'd done was listen to her messages.

Big mistake.

Chase pulled a bottled water out for himself and twisted off the cap. "So what's up? Nothing went wrong at the barn after we left, did it?"

"No." Chase and Josie had hung in, helping with the breakdown until the bitter end, when the last caterer had put the last box of empty champagne glasses back into their vans. "Thanks for staying, by the way. You were a big help with Nikki."

"No problem. She's giving you hives these days, I know, but I like the little brat." He took a swig of the water. "So...you were going to tell me what's happened?"

The subtle prompt surprised her. He was ordinarily the most patient of all men. He'd seen her through a lifetime of crises, and he'd never pushed. When Trent left, Chase had sat beside her in silence for hours, holding her hand and waiting for her to feel like talking.

And that was another off note. He *wasn't* sitting beside her. He wasn't holding her hand. He was still behind the bar.

She shifted on the sofa nervously. What was she missing?

She picked up a feather that lay on the arm of the sofa. She fingered it absently, using it to stall. If he had problems of his own tonight, she didn't want to add to them. She could always tell him about Dean Pitcher's message tomorrow.

She stroked the feather, pulling the vane softly until it lay smooth against its shaft. It wasn't a big feather, but it was a pretty one. A glossy, blue-and-green peacock feather.

Her hands froze as she realized what she was holding.

It was a feather from the dream catcher Josie had worn in her hair tonight.

Suddenly everything made sense. Susannah understood, finally, exactly what she had interrupted.

Slowly, she let her gaze rise to meet his.

"Chase? Is there anything you want to tell me?"

He didn't look guilty, didn't flush, didn't rush into over eager explanations. But he at least paid her the compliment of not denying it, of not pretending that she was being a typical paranoid female and imagining things.

"Not really, Sue. There's nothing to tell, nothing important, anyhow. It was a momentary madness."

"But…if she…if you—"

"Don't let it upset you," he said with a wry smile. "It might scare *me* a little—I honestly thought I was smarter than that. But there's nothing about it that should scare *you*. It didn't go very far."

"It didn't?" She tried to return his smile. "Saved by the bell, so to speak?"

"More or less." He ran his hand through his hair. "All I can say is…please don't let it worry you. She's going home on Monday."

He looked miserable. He shouldn't have let it come to this, and he would know that better than anyone. He'd hate it. He'd hate having to accept that he wasn't perfect, that he wasn't strong enough to do the right thing at all times.

Oh, God, what a mess.

Suddenly she remembered how sympathetic her friend Dina Waters had been to her tonight. Dina had teasingly asked Susannah if the minidress was the new romance strategy. "Gotta make sure Chase doesn't fall for the pretty little friend from out of nowhere?"

Susannah had found that amusing. How dumb Dina was, she'd thought. Anyone with half a brain knew that you couldn't catch Chase with bait like miniskirts and S and M boots. He didn't go all drooly and brain-dead at the sight of a half-naked woman.

And why would she need to worry, anyhow? There was nothing between Chase and the pretty little friend from nowhere.

What a fool she was! Just as big a fool as she'd always been. All those years ago, Susannah had been the last to know that Trent was cheating on her. And apparently she hadn't learned a thing. She was still the last to know.

She set the feather carefully down on the arm of the sofa. The real question was…now what?

Here were the new facts. The new reality. Chase and Josie were in the middle of a serious chemistry attack. They had already reached the point of shedding feathers together on the couch.

If Susannah hadn't shown up when she did…

Was he even telling her the full truth? Had she actually shown up in time? And did it really matter? So what if Chase had become Josie Whitford's lover? Chase and Susannah were friends, no more than that. The marriage was a business deal. A favor. She might wish he wouldn't embarrass her by sleeping around, but if he did, so be it.

On the other hand, this tomcat behavior wasn't like him. When he had casual relationships, they were always with women who knew the script. He never messed around with women too naive or too needy to understand exactly what he was offering.

Josie Whitford was both of those things. To the max.

So what if…what if Josie really meant something special to him? If that were true, did it mean Susannah had to bow out? Was she required to jump up, full of generosity and self-denial, and hand Chase over to Josie with a smile?

Damn it, no. She might have liked to be a saint, a heroine who would conveniently die of consumption or get hit by a bus just when the hero needed to be released. But she wasn't a saint. She was a worried, tired woman scrabbling hard to save her business, save her home and save her little sister.

Chase's promise to Susannah only lasted one year. Even if Josie had fallen deeply in love with her newfound hero, couldn't she wait one measly year?

Susannah heard how selfish that attitude was, but she couldn't make herself care. She had to ensure that Chase understood Susannah's situation was desperate. Just as dire as any foolish girl who'd gotten herself pregnant by a cad charading as Chase.

"Chase…the reason I came." She swallowed hard. "I got a message tonight, from Dean Pitcher."

"Oh, yeah?" Chase's voice was somber. He knew that Susannah had been holding her breath, waiting to see if Pitcher, her primary buyer, was going to be able to honor his contracts for this year's crops.

"Yeah. He said he wanted to be the one to tell me. He's going out of business. Apparently all the rumors were true." She tried to give Chase a brave smile, but she was so tired, and the news had hit her so hard.

"He said he was sorry. Which was very nice, of course, but it won't…" She had to fight for a steady voice. "Won't find a home for my peaches."

Finally, Chase came out from behind the bar and sat beside her on the couch. Finally, he took hold of her hand. It almost made her cry, because it was such a familiar comfort. And she had needed it so much.

"It's okay," he said. "We'll find another

buyer. And when we sell off that west acreage, you'll have a little cushion again. Things won't seem so impossible."

She shook her head.

He touched her chin. "You'll make it, Sue. It won't be long now."

Not long until their wedding, that was what he meant. She leaned her head into his shoulder, relieved that there was no trace of ambivalence on his face, or in his voice.

But of course that was part of his code. He would never ask to be released from his promise. Directly or indirectly. She would never know what was in his heart. If he suffered, he would suffer in silence.

And still, selfish bitch that she was, she couldn't offer to set him free.

"I'm so sorry, Chase," she said. "I know it's a lot to ask. But the truth is, I need your help now more than ever."

WHEN SUSANNAH FINALLY went home, Chase walked slowly upstairs, dragging his hand along the banister, weariness filling his legs with lead.

He'd rather fall into his bed, fully dressed, and let sleep take him away. But this was something that had to be done.

He knocked on the guest room door.

Josie answered quickly. She was already in her nightgown. He'd bought her that nightgown—it seemed like so long ago. He'd bought it way back when he hadn't even considered how the strap would slide off her too-thin shoulder, or how the linen would hint at the outline of her breasts.

"Hi," she said. Her voice was soft and slightly nervous. He wondered what she thought he had come for. He wondered if she'd been waiting for him.

"I wanted to say I'm sorry about what happened. I have no excuses. I wanted you, and I didn't even try very hard to stop myself."

"I know," she said. "I— It was the same for me."

Her face was very pale. Just behind her, the moonlight was pooling on the white canopy bed. If he let himself imagine the way she would look, lying under him, with the ivory glow on her fair skin, he would go crazy.

So he didn't. He shut off the pictures. Turned off the tap that fed the fantasies.

"It was a terrible mistake," he said. "It wasn't fair to you. And it caused me to hurt someone I love very much."

"Susannah?"

"Yes. She trusted me. She always has. And I let her down." He took a deep breath. "You know Susannah and I are getting married next month."

Josie nodded. "To save her ranch."

"Yes, to save her ranch. And I could jump on that technicality, and use it to write my ticket to freedom. Sue and I aren't in love, Josie. We aren't lovers, and the marriage won't change that."

"I know."

"I suspect that, if I asked her, she would give me permission to take someone else into my bed. She doesn't require fidelity of me. But, the problem is, I require it of myself."

Her eyes were very round and dark.

He grabbed the door frame and held on tight, as if those eyes might draw him into her spell. Sometimes she was just a graceful, laughing girl who made his heart feel light.

And sometimes, like now, she was the most haunting woman he'd ever met.

"I want you, Josie. God knows, I want you so much I don't know how I'm going to be able to sleep. But I'm not going to come in, even if you would let me."

She didn't answer. He knew he should turn away and leave, but he wanted...more. Something he could hang on to. He wanted to hear her voice. He wanted to hear that she understood, that she wouldn't hate him the way he hated himself.

"Josie?"

She still didn't say anything. He wondered if she was trying not to cry. But wait...damn it, that was pretty damn ego-tistical. More likely she was just trying to stop herself from slapping him.

He wouldn't blame her. He was being a first-class ass. Seesawing between this fake Prince Valiant purity and tossing her onto the sofa for a quick tumble.

"Look, I'm not saying I'm perfect. I've been fighting myself almost every minute since I met you." He rubbed his hand across his brows. "Does this make sense to you at all? Damn it, Josie. Tell me what you're thinking."

"I'm thinking," she said, "that I wish the Chase Clayton I met had been even half the man you are." She smiled sadly. "But most of all, I'm thinking I wish I'd met you first."

CHAPTER FIFTEEN

THE DAY OF THE AUCTION preview was overcast and chilly, a marked contrast to the balmy spring days that preceded it. Josie borrowed one of Chase's jackets, and when she put it on she got a poignant twist in her midsection. It smelled like him, and that was a smell she would always associate with unfulfilled longing.

The preview was being held at a local auction house, and the field was crowded with sheds and tents, round pens for showing and arenas for riding. Consignors, buyers, staff, vets and food vendors bustled about, giving the whole thing a circus atmosphere.

Chase and Josie ambled around the edges, stopping now and then to look at horses he liked, or to talk to owners he knew. He filled her in on interesting tidbits about the horses—who actually seemed a lot like people, she thought. Some were mean, some were sociable, some born to be great, and others spoiled by bad training. Some of them even had obsessive-compulsive disorders, brought about by stress or boredom.

Chase seemed to know everyone. He couldn't go ten feet without being stopped by a backslap or a howdy. Josie noticed that he made a point of introducing her to every male under forty. Every time, she'd catch his eye, and subtly shake her head.

Sometimes she strolled behind him, just for the pleasure of watching him walk and talk and laugh with his friends. He was such a comfortable person, at home in his body and in his identity. He had only one manner—warm and down-to-earth. He treated rich, beautiful female owners exactly the same as he treated gap-toothed, wizened old horse handlers.

And clearly everyone loved him.

"I think I'll get Doc Blaiser to look at the radiographs on White Tornado here," he said after he'd spent about ten minutes with an impressive palomino. He pulled out his cell phone and began punching in numbers, obviously hoping to track down the vet. "It may take a while. Do you want to wait, or maybe just wander around a little?"

"I guess I'll look around."

"Good." He smiled. "Let me know if you run into any old friends."

She waved goodbye, then took off on her own, forcing herself not to look back. It was hard, though, to give up even a minute of this, her last day with him.

She knew she should be glad he'd come to his senses last night. She certainly hadn't been capable of pulling back on her own. Thanks to his willpower, she'd been spared the humiliation of being bedded, then abandoned, by Chase Clayton not just once, but twice.

But she wasn't glad. She would have given almost anything to have even that one foolish night with him.

As impossible as it sounded, she had fallen in love with this man.

She'd fallen in love with his eyes, his voice, his gentle hands. With his natural leadership, unquestioned by anyone on his ranch, from the horses to the cowboys. With his indifference to his millions, and his joy in simple things, like windswept nights filled with the cry of owls.

She'd fallen in love with his confidence, his laughter, his generosity. With his powerful, unstoppable instinct to safeguard the helpless.

And of course, with his bone-melting sex appeal.

It wasn't anything she could explain or defend. She would be ashamed even to say the words out loud, considering how foolish she'd been just three months ago, falling for the impostor.

But logic had no power over her. She loved him. And, as she moved into this scary, uncertain future, she would have cherished the memory of that one night.

Instead, she would have to make do with

this one last, rainy, politely distant day at the auction.

She stopped to look at a dapple gray, partly because its markings were so lovely, and partly because its shed seemed to be crowded with people. She scanned each face covertly, while she pretended to look at the distinctive green hats and key chains offered as giveaways by the sponsoring farm.

No one looked familiar. She started to elbow her way out, but one of the green-shirted staff stopped her, urging her to take a key chain. She clearly wasn't going to escape until she did. So she pocketed one, thanking the man, and made her way back out to the open arena.

She glanced back toward the palomino's shed, but Chase was already gone. She wondered how long it would take to look at the X-rays. Would he buy that beautiful horse? Or would the radiographs reveal a defect, a bone spur, maybe, or a cyst?

The secret flaw hiding inside the other-wise perfect animal.

And, however much he might have liked

the horse, Chase would walk away. He would have no choice.

She wandered aimlessly for at least twenty minutes, looking at a dozen horses, before she encountered a section of vendors showing off their bits and halters, saddles, supplements and stable supplies. Some tables invited you to join riding clubs. Others offered dressage lessons, pony rides for birthday parties, Western wear or silver belt buckles the size of dinner plates.

One table advertised a rodeo. Out of habit, she picked up their brochure, which was thick with color photos of bucking broncs and cowboys with their arms in the air and their hats flying out behind them.

She flipped through it perfunctorily. She had looked at so many cowboy faces in the past two weeks. They were all beginning to look the same.

And then, on the second page, it happened.

She saw him.

She paused, wondering if she was hallucinating. Then she squinted, holding the picture up closer, wondering if she was wrong.

It was hard to be sure. Objectively, his face was just a button-sized collection of grainy pixels rather poorly reproduced. He looked a little like Alexander Clayton, and a little like Chase himself. Heck, he even looked a little like the cowboy manning the rodeo table right now. Young, blond, male...

Objectively, it wasn't possible to be sure.

But her body knew. Her heart began to beat faster, and her hand began to shake.

She turned blindly. She had to find Chase. She squeezed the brochure so hard it bent in her hand, and she began to run.

She spotted him only ten feet from the palomino's tent. He saw her coming, and instinctively he frowned. He began to lope toward her.

"What's wrong?" He grabbed her arm. "Is it the baby?"

"No," she said. She held out the brochure. "It's Chase."

WHILE CHASE MADE CALLS, Josie waited in the kitchen of the Double C. She sat at the large table in the breakfast alcove, holding on to a large mug of hot tea.

Imogene had made it for her, to help her settle her nerves. For the first few minutes, the housekeeper had hovered a bit, offering sandwiches and sweaters, and the occasional gentle "It'll be fine, darling. Things always turn out fine in the end."

But finally she'd seemed to sense that Josie would rather be alone.

"I guess I'll do the living room flowers," she'd said reluctantly. "But if you need me, just holler. I'll be back in a flash."

When she was gone, Josie stared out the bay window, where the horses were playing tag and the gardeners were planting something bold and red. Someone was delivering large brown boxes to the ranch manager's office, just on the other side of the paddock.

She liked watching the routine of the Double C plod on. It was strangely comforting to see how little impact her personal drama had on the rest of the world.

No matter what Chase learned about the cowboy in the brochure, none of this clock-work efficiency would stop. The ranch would go on. It would thrive.

And so, somehow, would she.

She touched her stomach tentatively. She could feel a change there, a slight roundness. It felt solid, firm to the touch—which was somehow reassuring. It made the baby feel less fragile. Less dependent on its mother, who had no idea how to take care of it yet.

It gave her hope that, in the end, she could do this without screwing up. No matter how confused her head and heart might be, her body knew what to do. It was already preparing a safe cocoon in which the baby could grow.

She let her hand relax, resting over the bump. She cupped her palm across the curve, and massaged it slightly with her fingers.

"I'm here," she whispered. "I don't know about Daddy, but I will always be here."

A few minutes later, she heard Chase coming down the hall. She gave her belly one last, encouraging touch, and then she straightened her back and turned to face the door.

She knew just by looking at his face. They had found him.

"His name is Anthony Maguire," he said without preamble. "I know him. I fired him two years ago, for mistreating one of my horses."

She squeezed her hands together in her lap. Her heart was beating too fast, and she needed somehow to slow it down.

"Are you sure?"

"Yes. We talked to the rodeo company. He hasn't worked for them in quite a while. This picture is from a year ago. But they have the photo release form he signed at the time."

He tossed the brochure onto the table. Then he sat in the chair next to her and took her hands. "It has to be him, Josie. Do you have any idea what kind of coincidence it would take for you to ID one random rodeo cowboy picture out of the thousands floating around this county, only to find out this one used to work for me?"

She nodded. Intellectually, she understood. But emotionally…it simply didn't seem possible.

"The truth is, after so many failures, I'd sort of begun to believe I'd imagined him."

He smiled. He still held on to her hands. "I know. I sometimes wished you had, too. But unfortunately, the facts were always there, proving he was real-life flesh and blood."

"Yes." She thought of the tiny life, floating inside her, perhaps sensing Josie's heartbeat like the strange pulsing of a distant moon. And she couldn't be sorry. Whatever else this man did to her, he had left her with this gift, this miracle that was better than either of them could ever be.

Chase tightened his grip on her hands. "Tell me what you want to do."

That, of course, was the ultimate question.

What *did* she want to do? Everything felt different now. When she'd first discovered she was pregnant, she'd been angry and sick. And afraid. So afraid.

She'd had only one thought. To find him, and make him own up to his sins. And pay for them, too. In cold hard cash, if possible.

She had wanted to force him to save her. One way or another.

But then she'd met the real Chase, and somehow he had taught her how to save herself. He'd taught her what real strength looked like. And real love, too. He'd taught her what it felt like to really love a man.

And what it felt like to love herself.

Today, the idea of hunting this man down like a dog, of bringing him to his knees...none of those things felt quite the same.

"What did you say his name was?"

"Anthony Maguire."

She said the name over in her mind, trying it on. It was hard to make the switch. "Why didn't you recognize him from the sketch the artist made? It wasn't perfect, but it was close."

"Maguire didn't look like this when he

worked for me. For one thing, he's lost about forty or fifty pounds, I'd say. He was never a very tall guy, but he was a good bit overweight. And he's changed his hair—dyed it, definitely. He used to be brunette. And he used to have a beard."

She frowned. "But that's—so much change…that almost has to be deliberate."

"Yeah," he said. "I think so, too. But it doesn't have to be criminal. Maybe he just wanted to reinvent himself. He wasn't very well liked when he was here. He was always putting on airs, they say, always acting as if he was better than the other hands."

"Do you remember him well?"

"Not really. Trent had to remind me about that part. All I remember is finding him and a couple of other guys one day, racing three of my best horses out in the south pastures. They hadn't asked permission, they just decided it would be fun. This guy was on Alcatraz, and using his whip like a madman. Hand up above his shoulder, stabbing down, hitting over and over, till he drew blood."

"Oh, my God."

"Yeah. I fired all three of them, but Maguire got the worst of it. I didn't hold back, not even a little." He shook his head. "I'm not surprised the guy hates me. And frankly, the feeling is mutual."

He drummed his fingers on the tabletop, and stared out through the bay window, as if remembering all the drama of that day. Josie tried to picture the man she'd known as Chase. She tried to imagine his hands holding the riding crop and beating the horse with it.

The same hands that had touched her.

She felt her stomach tighten, and a rush of morning sickness, the first in days, moved through her.

"I need to know what you want to do, Josie. Obviously he has to be stopped. And if he has any assets, he should be forced to help out with the baby. But do you want to get involved in that personally? I can always sic Stilling on him. Establishing paternity shouldn't be difficult. There are legal avenues that wouldn't require you to lay eyes on him, if you didn't want to."

She hesitated. What was the wise choice? What, in the end, would be best for her child? Was money that important? Would even a million dollars be worth it, if it meant bringing a lying, violent bastard into their lives?

"I want to see him," she said. "I want to look into his eyes one more time, now that I know…the truth. And then I'll decide what to do."

CHAPTER SIXTEEN

IT WAS, CHASE THOUGHT, like finding the right combination to a safe. Once they had a name, the steel door swung open, and the rest of the information cascaded into their hands.

Four hours later, the bastard was theirs.

Ironically, he lived in San Antonio. They had probably been within five miles of him the day they came to check out Alexander.

His house looked much like the others on his street. Small, ordinary, well kept. A few azaleas, looking their best right about now, and a satellite dish on the roof.

You sure couldn't tell from the exterior that a scumbag lived inside.

As they reached the front stoop, they heard the television droning through the half-open window. A little Honda, not too old—not even as old as Josie's car had been, sat in the carport, so they were pretty sure the bastard was home.

Chase glanced at Josie. She appeared surprisingly calm. Maybe she was numb. She'd been very quiet on the drive over.

"You ready?" He gave her a smile.

"Ready enough," she said. And then, taking one deep breath, she lifted her hand and knocked on the door.

First the television grew quiet, and then the thin door opened. A pretty young blonde with shoulder-length hair and a lot of freckles stood there, one hand on the doorknob and the other on her stomach.

Her very pregnant stomach.

Chase felt Josie go utterly still.

"Hi," the woman said. She scanned them quickly, as if trying to decide whether they might be selling something. "Can I help you?"

Josie's face seemed frozen. She was smiling, but it was like an image caught on a computer monitor that had already lost its power. It wasn't happening in real time.

"We're looking for Anthony Maguire," Chase said, quickly covering the pause. "Is this his house?"

"Yes." The woman's light, curving brows knitted. "I'm Tony's wife. Bonnie. Can I help you?"

The woman clearly wasn't the defiant type, but she wasn't an idiot, either. She had no intention of telling them anything else until she had some idea what was going on. Chase thought it was quite possible she'd opened the door to strangers with bad news before.

Bill collectors, maybe?

Other girlfriends?

Actually, she looked like a nice woman, with round, girlish features and an innocent expression in her brown eyes. Too bad she'd picked such a louse to marry.

And have kids with.

Josie finally spoke up. "Is Anthony at home?"

The other woman cocked her head. "I'm sorry—I don't think I caught your name."

"I'm Chase Clayton." He smiled. "Tony used to work for me."

Josie made a jerky movement, but before she could protest he reached in his pocket and pulled out one of his cards. He held it out to the woman in the doorway.

"It was three years ago. I don't think you guys were married then."

She studied the card, turning it over as if she wanted to be hard-nosed and skeptical, but obviously impressed by the embossed Double C brand.

"No," she said. She seemed to relax now that she knew he wasn't a lawyer or a bill collector. "We've only been married two years. But if you'll come in, Mr. Clayton, I'm sure Tony will—"

Her soft Texas drawl was interrupted by a gruff male voice.

"I'll handle this, Bonnie," the man said.

Bonnie glanced over her shoulder. "Are you sure, honey? If you need to rest, I can bring them into the living room and—"

"I'll take care of it."

With a worried, slightly embarrassed

smile, the woman bowed out, making room for the man to take her place.

As soon as he came into sight, Josie's paralyzed silence ended. She made a small, disbelieving sound.

Chase came close to doing the same thing. The man who stood before them had the blond hair and the blue eyes Josie had described. But the rest of his face...

The rest was hardly human.

"LOOK, I'M NOT defending myself," Anthony Maguire said dully. "I told you I don't blame you for being angry."

Josie watched him shift his weight on his crutches, trying to get comfortable. It was difficult to see him struggle so hard without wanting to look away.

With one of his legs in a cast up to the thigh, it had taken forever for them to walk down to Chase's truck. But Anthony had insisted on doing so. Obviously he hadn't wanted his wife to hear the conversation he knew was coming.

Josie had walked just in front of him, so

that she didn't have to look at him, or risk touching him. From the left profile, he appeared almost the same. But from the right side, where the bronc had trampled him, the entire shape of his cheek and jaw was wrong.

Hideous.

But also pitiful.

They'd been down here for almost ten minutes now, listening in shocked silence while Anthony described the rodeo accident that had left him so broken and disfigured.

It had happened just a few days after he left Josie. Finally she learned why he'd bolted from Riverfork, ditching Josie without even a goodbye call.

After several months of being estranged, his wife had called him. Bonnie wanted to try again.

This time they could make it work, she'd said. This time they had a good enough incentive. She was going to have a baby.

When she heard that, Josie glanced at Chase. She couldn't read his expression. Like her, he seemed reluctant to speak.

Neither of them wanted to break the flow of the other man's story.

Apparently the rodeo had been Anthony's income, ever since he was fired from the Double C. He did all right, he said. Not great, but enough to buy this little house.

He'd always been fairly conservative, balancing his physical safety with his need to earn a living. But when he and Bonnie had separated, he'd decided to go for broke. And he'd won big. Right around Christmas, he was golden, winning everything he entered.

That was the money he'd used to impress Josie. He'd blown it all in one month. He shrugged. It wasn't cheap to pull off an impersonation of a millionaire.

"I guess that's why most people don't even try," Chase said drily.

There was a pause, in which Josie could see Anthony's hands flexing and unflexing on the handle of the crutch.

"Most people haven't had to spend a year kissing the ground at the great Chase Clayton's feet." For the first time, Anthony sounded belligerent. "The way I saw it, you owed me."

"I owe you, all right," Chase said. "I owe you a little vacation in the county jail."

"Don't take that superior tone with me, Clayton. I'm not a fool. Nothing I did was illegal. I didn't steal anything from you. I didn't use your precious credit cards or your bank accounts. I just borrowed a little of the glow that comes with being a Clayton."

"Interesting distinction. What do you say we take it to a judge or two, and see what they think?"

"And the judges would just happen to be your drinking buddies, right?" Anthony laughed harshly. "You people are so goddamn corrupt."

Josie saw a pulse jump in Chase's jaw. She touched his elbow, which was as hard as a rock. She squeezed it softly, just to remind him that she was here.

The connection helped her to focus, too. She forced herself to look at Anthony, hoping her horror didn't show too clearly on her face.

"So how did you get hurt? I mean, if the rodeos were going so well..."

Anthony looked back at her. He smiled, horribly, through the unnatural jaw, connected with metal plates. His nose had been broken, and his cheekbone sagged under his right eye. The imprint of a horseshoe branded his right cheek, and everywhere searing scars crisscrossed the once-smooth skin.

Somewhere in all that, she could almost glimpse the handsome man who had so suavely romanced her. But it was like finding the singed corner of a letter buried in the ashes of a fire. It only accented the loss.

"The luck always changes, Josie. *Always.* You know that. I'd taken a month off, the month I spent with you. I wasn't in the greatest shape. But with a baby on the way, Bonnie and I needed the money. So I gambled, hoping for the big purse."

He shrugged. "And I lost. Big-time. The bronc went nuts, I hit the ground, and I've been drinking soup and milk through a straw ever since. And, of course, the morphine. Thank *God* for the morphine."

She opened her mouth—but his story had snatched the words right out of her throat. Even though the entire trip to San Antonio had been spent practicing how she would show him her contempt, suddenly she couldn't utter a single syllable.

He had done terrible things, both to her and to Chase. But was there any point in trying to punish him anymore?

Fate had tracked him down far faster than she could.

And Fate had laid him low.

"So let me guess." Chase didn't appear to be similarly moved. "Now I guess you expect us to say, hey, no problem, it's all good—just because you went and got yourself trampled?"

Anthony laughed, low and tight. "No way, boss man. Not you. Remember, I've seen your particular brand of justice, and it lacks a certain, shall we say...*mercy?*"

"Sure. Let's say that. I show no mercy to lying, vicious sons of bitches. That's something I can live with. You show no mercy to innocent young women, one of whom is unfortunate enough to actually be married to you. And even, God help her, carrying your—"

Josie demurred softly. Hearing it, Chase stopped himself short. He turned to her. "Okay. Once again, Josie, it's up to you. What do you want to do with this pathetic weasel?"

Anthony moved forward, hopping on his one good foot.

"Listen," he said roughly. "I don't care what you do. All I ask is that, if we're going to have to tell Bonnie, let me be the one to do it."

Chase ignored him. "Josie? What's it going to be? Just say the word, and we can squash this bastard like a bug."

She pretended to think a little, though in reality her mind was already made up. Bonnie loved him. Bonnie probably was the only thing in the world that stood between Anthony Maguire and true despair.

And there was Bonnie's baby…

And he wasn't going to be masquerading as Chase again any time soon. The next young woman he approached was far more likely to scream than swoon.

"Look at him," she said. "I'd say he's already been effectively neutralized, wouldn't you? Anything we did now would be overkill."

"Damn it, Josie." Chase narrowed his eyes. "Are you sure? No matter what he says, the law is on your side, in every way. There's nothing you'd like to tell him?"

She shook her head firmly, hoping Chase would get the message. "Nothing."

"And nothing you want *from* him? Not a dime? Not even a little revenge?"

"Not one single thing," she said. She held out her hand. "Come on. Let's get out of here."

ON THE DRIVE HOME, they didn't even try to maintain a sensible distance. He pulled her up against him, wrapped his arm around her slender, shaking shoulders, and let her weep into his shirt.

It was good for her, he knew. She'd misted up a few times, but through this whole ordeal he'd never seen her really break down. She was overdue for a good cry.

And besides, this morning had been hell. Even Chase had been moved by the sight of that poor bastard, with his face all stomped to hell. He could only imagine how it had affected Josie. After all, just a few months ago she had found Maguire charming enough to…

But Chase didn't really like to think about that. Even while he was feeling sorry for Anthony Maguire, he had been fighting the primitive male urge to beat the guy to raw meat, just because he'd had the nerve to put his dirty hands on Josie.

How caveman was that? Apparently civilization was a pretty thin veneer covering over some fairly primitive emotions.

But he hadn't done it. That was something, right? He hadn't done it because Maguire was already such a mess—and because Josie hadn't wanted him to.

She had such a forgiving nature. He

knew that she was crying now not so much for herself and her lost dream, but for Maguire's pain. And maybe for that poor little rag doll wife of his.

Chase stroked the side of Josie's head, running his fingers along the silk of her hair. Now and then he'd smooth the tears away from her cheek. He murmured soft noises that didn't really mean anything— except that he understood.

But though they were intense, the tears didn't last long. He had just barely pulled his car onto Interstate 35 heading north when she lifted her head.

"I'm sorry," she said, pulling a tissue out to wipe her eyes. "I think it's—"

"I know," he said. "You don't have to explain. You've kept a lot of stuff bottled up inside. It's good to let it out."

She nodded. "I guess so."

He pulled her back down to his shoulder. She resisted for a second, and then she let herself relax against him. They drove that way for a long time, in silence, while the motels, and gas stations and all the

unlovely hodgepodge of a city's outskirts
rolled by on either side.

He knew she might be hungry, and he
thought about stopping. But a low-level
anxiety kept drumming through his veins.
Sooner or later, she was going to start
talking again about going home.

He wanted to prevent that. If he could
just get her back to the Double C, where
he knew she had begun to feel at home,
he'd feel safer. Imogene would feed her,
and pet her and generally baby her until
she felt better.

Maybe she could take a nap. And then,
when this morning's trauma had faded to
a more manageable distance, they could
sit on the porch and talk about what she
should do now.

They were about twenty minutes outside
Austin when his luck ran out.

"Chase," she said, lifting her head. "I
want to go home."

"We'll be there soon," he said.

"No. Not the ranch. My home."

"You want to drive all the way to River-fork tonight?"

She shook her head. "No. My parents live just south of Austin." She put the palm of her hand on his chest. "Can you take me there, Chase? I want to see my mother."

SUSANNAH WAS WAITING for Chase at the Double C. She wanted to get home and check on Nikki, but she couldn't bring herself to leave without hearing what had happened in San Antonio. So she kept in touch by cell phone, driving Nikki wild with frustration.

"I'm doing my homework, for God's sake. Get a life of your own, why don't you?"

By ten, Susannah had fallen asleep on the sofa. The sound of the banjo clock in the hall woke her up at eleven. And then again at midnight.

By twelve-thirty, just when she was starting to get really worried, she heard Chase's truck pull into the drive, its tires crunching slowly along the oyster-shell surface.

She jumped to her feet, smoothed her hair and her skirt and met him on the porch.

"Chase!" She reached up to give him a kiss, shocked by the drawn, tight lines of his tired face. "Did you find him?"

He nodded. "I'll tell you all about it tomorrow, okay, Sue? It's been a long day."

"But can't you tell me anything? Did he deny it? Are you going to file charges? Is he going to help Josie with the baby?"

"No," he said flatly, "no, and no." There was no point in denying it. "Josie didn't want me to prosecute. And as for helping…the man is a total wreck. He doesn't have the wits or the assets to help anybody, including himself."

Susannah's heart fell. She had so hoped that something good would come of this. Something that could make her feel less guilty about everything.

"Oh, poor Josie. How did she take it?"

He shrugged. "It was hard. But the girl's got grit. She's going to be fine."

"I'm sure she will." She looked out toward the truck. It seemed to be empty.

Could Josie be lying down, asleep on the seat? Maybe the long day had been too much for her, after last night's excitement. She was tons better, but she didn't have her full strength back yet.

"Can I help her with anything? Does she need something to eat? Imogene's asleep already, but I could—"

"No, Sue. She doesn't need anything." The porch light caught his eyes. They were as bleak as blue ice.

"Chase." Susannah's hands felt slightly cold. "Where is she?"

He shook his head. "She's gone."

CHAPTER SEVENTEEN

AFTER LUNCH THE NEXT DAY, Susannah drove her Jeep right up to the ranch manager's office, yanked on the emergency brake and killed the engine. She knew Trent was here. His Mercedes hugged the side of the building, the sleek machine drowsing elegantly under the warm sun. It even looked like him, she thought. Glamorous and bored on the outside, dangerously powerful and primitive on the inside.

She squared her shoulders, took a deep breath and set her jaw. Then she jumped down, before she could change her mind.

She didn't knock. She just shouldered open the door and walked straight past his secretary, all the way to his desk.

He looked up, with one sardonically

cocked eyebrow. *Of course*, she thought. He was far too cool to admit to being surprised to see her.

"Hey, there," he said. He slowly scanned her from head to toe, taking in the tailored shirt, the pleated linen slacks. "I liked your miniskirt better."

"I don't give a damn."

"I know." He smiled. "Is that all you wanted to say?"

"No." She decided to dispense with the whole prologue she'd created and just get to the point. The sooner she did, the sooner she could get out of here.

"I wanted to tell you…" She took another deep breath. "Chase is in love with Josie."

"That I also know." He shrugged. "Is there anyone who doesn't? Except perhaps Chase himself?"

"Maybe not. As you may remember, when it comes to things like this, I'm always the last to know."

"Yes." He smiled. "And the last to forgive, as well."

She felt her blood pressure rising. "Look, Trent. I don't have time for this."

He picked up his pen and started to sign one of the many documents that littered his desk. "Then by all means, don't let me keep you."

She growled softly under her breath. How did he do this to her every time? He was the only human being on earth who could make her lose her cool with just the slightest tweak of his tone, or angle of his eyebrow.

She reached out and wrapped her hand over the top of the pen, stalling its motion. "Damn it, you self-satisfied jerk. I need your help."

"With what?"

"With Chase."

Trent sat back in his big leather chair. He watched her through hooded eyes. "What do you need me to do?"

"I need you to marry me."

THE NEW RANCH HAND was clearly surprised to see Chase come into the south stables midafternoon, just about the time they were sending the family horses to the turnout pen.

"Do you need me to saddle up one of the horses, sir?" Richie had that eagerness that only the very young ever have for their jobs. "We've already turned out most of them, but I could—"

"No, that's fine." Chase waved him off. "I just felt like taking a look around."

The truth was, Chase found the whole aura of the stables comforting. It was such a simple place. Whitewashed wooden walls; wood shavings on the floors; uniform, roomy stalls. The tack hanging along the walls was the only decoration, but he'd take saddles and bridles over crystal and china any day.

In here, everything went according to schedule, and the horses were easy to please. Treat them fairly, feed them on time, give them plenty of fresh air and time to stretch their legs, and they'd do anything you asked them to do.

Captain Kirk was still in his stall. He was getting too old to run with the crowd, but someone rode him every day. Sometimes, Chase found time to do it, and when he didn't, he missed his time with the old guy.

He got close enough to the stall to let Captain Kirk nuzzle his jacket. The horse was spoiled, of course. He knew that Chase never showed up without bringing a treat.

"Okay. Which pocket?"

He had a carrot in his left, and one of Imogene's apple-and-oats cookies in the other. Captain Kirk had a sweet tooth, so he knew which one he wanted. He nuzzled at the right pocket, lifted his lip and nickered softly.

Chase's dad had been horrified when he realized that his young son let his new horse poke around his pockets. He thought it was a bad habit, and could lead to trouble down the road. But Chase had been lucky. Captain Kirk never pushed his boundaries, never nipped or got too pushy.

He fed the horse the cookie in small pieces, then dusted off his hands. "Yeah, you're a sweet old soul, aren't you, buddy?"

"Actually," Trent said from behind him, "I am. Thank you for noticing."

Chase chuckled. "Hey," he said. "What's up?"

Trent strolled up to the Dutch doors and gave Captain Kirk a good scratch on the withers.

"Not much," he said. "Two things, really. First, I'm just wondering how you're doing."

Chase pulled the carrot out of his pocket and concentrated on breaking it into pieces. The old Captain might prefer the cookie, but he'd never say no to a carrot. He'd developed quite an appetite in his old age.

"I'm fine," he said. "Got a lot to catch up on, of course. I didn't get much done while Josie was here."

Trent didn't answer right away. He just leaned against the stall and watched Chase feed the carrot to the horse. Finally he smiled. "Yeah. I can see you haven't got a second to spare."

Chase started to protest. But what was the use? Trent knew him too well.

He frowned. "Man, I need to get some new friends."

"You mean ones who don't know where the bodies are buried?" Trent put his hands in his pockets. "Naw, it would be too much work breaking them in. Much easier just to be honest about how you feel. It's got to feel weird, after having her living right in your house. She had something, didn't she?"

Chase had to be careful not to say too much. If he let himself, he could definitely disgrace the cowboy tradition of silent stoicism.

"Yeah. She definitely did have something. Now that she's gone, the house feels like…like someone pulled the power line down."

"Yeah. You've got a couple of ranch hands who are brokenhearted this morning. Apparently they worshipped her from afar. And Imogene sniffled all over the pancakes she brought out to us. I almost couldn't eat."

"I guess we'll all just have to get over it. I tried to get her to stay a little longer. She could get a job in town, if she's sick of being idle. It's crazy for her to go somewhere she isn't wanted, when—"

He stopped, hearing the intensity in his voice. Captain Kirk nuzzled his cheek sympathetically.

"It's okay," Trent said. "Heck, even I miss her."

Chase didn't want to think about it anymore. He felt like a man who was entering prison, or going to war. He was committed to Susannah for one year, one month and two days.

Until he'd served his time, he couldn't say a damn thing to Josie. He couldn't even ask her if she cared about him. Couldn't ask whether she'd even want to see him again, when the marriage was over.

And he certainly couldn't ask if she'd be willing to wait.

Bad enough that it would be rough on Sue, knowing that he was just counting the minutes until the cell doors clanged open. Much worse, it would be asking the impossible of Josie.

By the time he was free again, the baby would be about seven months old. Her pregnancy, her delivery, all of that would be endured alone. She couldn't wait that long to find someone to share her joys, share her burdens, share the miracle of the baby. She needed help now.

And as Trent had just pointed out, half the men who laid eyes on her would gladly volunteer for the task.

"So. You said you had two things. What is thing number two?"

Trent smiled serenely, looking exactly like the cat who had just swallowed the canary. "Oh, nothing big. I just came down to return something to you."

"What?"

Trent brought his hand out of his pocket. "This," he said. He stretched out his hand.

Curious, Chase held out his own. And then, with a little, glittering plop, Trent dropped a diamond ring into his palm.

"What the hell?" He turned the cool, platinum band over, checking out the distinctive square-cut chunk of white fire. It couldn't be…. He had to be imagining things. But it was.

He looked up. "This is Susannah's engagement ring."

"Not anymore," Trent said. "Sorry, pal, but we've had a change of plans."

JOSIE HADN'T SPENT A NIGHT under her stepfather's roof in seven years.

To her surprise, a lot had changed since then.

For one thing, Walter seemed to have mellowed a little.

He had always been a creature of routine. He liked his dinner on time, his home quiet and his wife at his beck and call. He liked to reign supreme over an orderly kingdom.

That part hadn't changed. When she showed up at his door, he wasn't happy to see her, and he didn't pretend to be. But he didn't say anything downright hostile or insulting, which was a marked contrast to the last time they'd met.

Of course, his civility might have been

because he was a little intimidated by Chase. It was one thing to berate your dependent child, in the privacy of your home, where you are the undisputed king. But it was something altogether different to show that side of yourself in front of a man of money, influence and great personal presence.

Maybe the most amazing change, though, was in her mother. For the first time, her mom seemed to have some fire inside. After Chase left, when Walter started holding forth about how irresponsible it was to create a child you couldn't support, Josie's mother touched his arm and said, "None of that, now. I'm thrilled about this baby."

It was offered in a gentle tone, and with a conciliatory smile, but, for Josie, it seemed to be a huge milestone. For the first time in her conscious life, Josie dared to hope her mother might become an ally.

And that was perfect timing. Because she could really use a friend.

She couldn't believe how much it hurt to lose Chase.

If she had ever wondered whether her feelings for the fake Chase had been love, she knew better now. When he disappeared from her life, she had been disappointed, embarrassed, even depressed.

But that was all.

This loss…this was something as different from that as the acorn is different from the oak. This emptiness hollowed out her heart, and throbbed inside her soul.

More than once, in that long first night, as she tried to sleep in the bed of her childhood, she considered calling him.

She had never told him that she loved him. She would do that now. She would tell him that, no matter what happened, she would wait for him.

Somehow she stopped herself from making that call. It was wrong on so many levels. First, the declaration would hang there, in the background of his relationship with Susannah, like a fog. They might never be able to see their way through that fog, and find each other.

She knew what Chase had said, but no

one could really predict what the future held for his marriage. He and Susannah intended for it to last only a year, a partnership between old friends, a way to save the orchard.

But what if something bigger should grow? What if some night, out of loneliness or need, they turned to each other and discovered love there, like violets growing unnoticed under a canopy of trees?

And what if, quite by accident, they found themselves with a baby on the way?

No, she couldn't be the invisible third party in their marriage. It wasn't fair to them—and it wasn't, in the end, even fair to herself. She needed to move on. She needed to find a way to make a life for the baby, a life that wasn't dependent on any man.

Not even her stepfather.

The minute she got up the next morning, she studied the classifieds. No more restaurant work. She needed a full-time job, an office job with health insurance, a steady paycheck and the kind of hours you could build a family around.

She filled out some online applications, faxed her résumé to a couple of places and phoned another. One legal office called back almost immediately, wanting to set up interviews.

It was encouraging. No one was offering a huge salary, but she was willing to start at the bottom.

She wished she could tell Chase about it. Surely it wouldn't be evil just to call him as a friend, just to tell him about the progress.

Evil? Maybe not. But foolish? Definitely.

She put the phone down and went out to join her mother in the garden.

The suburban yard wasn't the Double C, with its spreading acres of flowering trees and green fields, but her mother's backyard bed was a forty-by-twenty-foot work of art.

During Josie's growing-up years, she had resented the hours her mother spent out here, planting phlox, fertilizing columbine. She had always refused to help, even when her mother asked.

But now she finally understood some things a little better. Even her mother. She saw that her mother had needed some time to herself, a place where she was the queen, instead of merely the handmaiden to the king.

Obviously, Ellen Whitford hadn't been the perfect mother. But maybe she'd been as good as she knew how to be.

Josie climbed down the back stairs and crossed the perfectly trimmed green lawn. She knelt next to her mother and picked up the orange-handled weeder. "Shall I help get these dandelions out of here?"

Her mother wasn't big on discussing emotion, but her expression was thanks enough.

"Okay, then," Josie said, squeezing her mother's hand. "Let's get this done."

They spent two hours out there, until the sun dipped far enough to make the house cast long, olive-green rectangles on the grass. They talked more honestly than Josie could ever remember talking to her mother. It filled one of the empty places in Josie's heart. She wondered if it had done the same for her mother.

They both had difficulties to face. They were both trying to find the courage it would take. Maybe they could help each other along the way.

As the shadows grew closer, and eventually nipped at their heels, they decided to call it a day.

Her mother went inside first, nervously saying something about getting dinner started in time. Josie let it pass. Her mother's relationship was too complicated for her to fully understand—and besides, it was really not her business. Something had kept the two together all these years.

And although Josie wouldn't have wanted a lifetime of anxious servility, she did understand the longing for security, for the comfort of knowing someone would always be there.

Maybe someday she would find that.

When she thought the words, she tried to force herself not to think of Chase. She tried to leave a blank where the "someone" should be—tried to leave an opening that would give some man a chance.

But she couldn't. The only someone she wanted was the one she'd left behind.

She stayed outdoors a few more minutes, enjoying the last of the sunlight. She sat cross-legged in the dirt, the knees of her jeans black with earth, and her fingernails dark all the way down to the quick.

And then she saw a new shadow, moving around the side of the house. This one was tall, and narrow, and walking directly toward her.

Her heart skipped a beat, though she tried to settle it down. Why was she such a dreamer? It was probably her stepfather, or maybe a neighbor....

But her heart knew better. It picked up its pace, until by the time the shadow cleared the house, her pulse was speeding so fast she could hardly breathe.

She rose to her feet, dropping the weeder into the mulch.

"Chase!"

He didn't say a word, not even her name. He just took her in his arms, and he kissed her, the way she had always dreamed of being kissed. She didn't even think of re-sisting. It was something she had to do, like taking a breath of air after swimming a long time under water.

She put her arms up and ran her fingers through his hair. His lovely, golden hair.

Finally, he released her lips, though he still held her tightly against him.

"I have something to tell you, Josie," he said. "And I don't care how crazy it sounds, or how impossible it seems."

"Neither do I," she said with a shaky smile. "In fact, I have quite recently begun to believe in impossible things."

"Then believe this. I love you. I tried to let you go. I know you have decisions to make, and problems to face. I'm asking you to face them with me."

"But—"

He shook his head. "If you say one more word about how you can't accept my charity, I'll go mad. This isn't about you needing me, Josie. This is about me needing you. The truth is that I cannot live without you."

She hadn't been about to say anything of the sort. The joy of being in his arms made thinking very difficult. She hadn't been able to move past the one big obstacle, the same one that had been between them from the beginning.

"What about Susannah?"

His face sobered. "Unfortunately, she has decided she can't marry me after all. She's had a better offer."

Josie laughed. "Now I know you're lying. A better offer? There is no such thing."

"For Susannah there is," he said, his eyes sparkling. "She's going to marry the man she's loved since she was twelve years old. She's going to marry Trent."

"Trent? But everybody knows that Susannah… well, I don't know how else to put it. Imogene told me that Susannah *hates* Trent!"

"That's true, too," he admitted. "It's a very tangled relationship. But that's what will make it fun."

"Can you be sure, though, that she really wants this? Maybe she's just trying to set you free. Maybe she suspected that something was going on between us. When she came to the house, after the dance—"

"She knew, of course. She understands me pretty well, and it's hard to fool her. She knew I'd fallen in love with you. I'm sure that's why she broke down and proposed to Trent."

She searched his face, which was glowing in the golden light of the sinking sun. Behind him, the amaryllis were blazing, as if they were on fire.

"Are you okay with that? You don't feel guilty about letting her down? You're not worried that she might feel...abandoned?"

"Nope. I've just put her in the hands of a man who adores her. I've just given her a chance to get her life right. I don't see how a best friend could possibly be asked to do more than that."

He grinned. "Besides, if I try to change things now, Trent will never forgive me. He's been waiting for this miracle for ten whole years."

She didn't know what to say. She hated

to let herself believe it could be true. The idea that Susannah's needs no longer took precedence over hers...

"I can't believe it," she said.

"It's true, though. Trent may have been waiting for Susannah for ten years. But I've been waiting my whole life for you. Please say yes, Josie. Say you'll come back to the Double C."

"I don't know." She didn't want to be sensible. She wanted to throw herself into his arms and drive off with him into the sunset. But she'd thrown caution to the winds once before, and look where that got her.

"I love you, Chase. I know that what I feel for you is real. But it's not just about me. I need to think of the baby, and the future. I have to be so careful."

He put his hand against her stomach. It was so warm and strong. She leaned into it instinctively. "When you first came to me, you thought I was your baby's father. Help me to make that come true. Let me be there for both of you, as a husband and a daddy, starting today—and lasting the rest of our lives."

"But—" she searched his face, looking for the truth "—are you really sure?"

"Absolutely." He leaned in and kissed her once, lightly. "I love you, Josie." He kissed her again. "I love you more than I've ever loved anything or anyone in my life."

The words went through her like a shimmer of sunlight. She smiled, and he kissed her yet again.

"More than your first wife, the legendary beauty?"

He laughed. "Yes, but that doesn't prove anything. She was also a legendary witch."

"More than all the pretty cowgirls I saw you dancing with at Susannah's party?"

"More than all of them," he said, kissing her more deeply this time. "And their sisters and cousins, too."

"Hmm." She wanted more kisses, so she had to think of more tests. "More than Big Muddies, and Imogene's hash browns? More than your truck?"

"You are food and drink to me now," he

said, and proved it by nibbling softly on her lower lip. "And I'd drive the truck into Clayton Creek if you asked me to."

"Ahh…" She tilted her head and smiled up at him. "More than Yipster, the world's nicest dog?"

"Hey, that's not fair!" He laughed out loud. "If you really want to test me, I know what we can do. Let's buy a new puppy for the baby, and then, in ten or fifteen years, you can ask me again."

Ten or fifteen years…

Well, it was a start.

She caught a glimpse of her mother on the back porch. She was wringing her hands, looking distressed. Then Josie saw why. Her stepfather was standing right behind her mother. His face was tight and disapproving.

"I have an even better test," she whispered. "My stepfather is about three more kisses away from storming out here and asking you what your intentions are."

Chase gave the porch a glance, then turned his gaze back to her. "My intentions are to marry you, and, if I can, to make ours the happiest family in Texas. He never loved you enough, Josie. But that's all right, because I intend to love you too much."

"You're actually going to tell him that?"

"I can't wait." He lowered his lips to hers. "So let's get him out here. Let's get started on those three kisses, Josie. Let's get started on forever."

* * * * *

2 FREE

BOOKS AND A SURPRISE GIFT!

We would like to take this opportunity to thank you for reading this Mills & Boon® book by offering you the chance to take TWO more specially selected titles from the Superromance series absolutely FREE! We're also making this offer to introduce you to the benefits of the Mills & Boon® Book Club™—

- ★ FREE home delivery
- ★ FREE gifts and competitions
- ★ FREE monthly Newsletter
- ★ Exclusive Mills & Boon Book Club offers
- ★ Books available before they're in the shops

Accepting these FREE books and gift places you under no obligation to buy, you may cancel at any time, even after receiving your free shipment. Simply complete your details below and return the entire page to the address below. You don't even need a stamp!

YES! Please send me 2 free Superromance books and a surprise gift. I understand that unless you hear from me, I will receive 4 superb new titles every month for just £3.69 each, postage and packing free. I am under no obligation to purchase any books and may cancel my subscription at any time. The free books and gift will be mine to keep in any case.

U9ZED

Ms/Mrs/Miss/Mr .... Initials ....
BLOCK CAPITALS PLEASE

Surname ....

Address ....

....

.... Postcode ....

Send this whole page to:
UK: FREEPOST CN81, Croydon, CR9 3WZ

Offer valid in UK only and is not available to current Mills & Boon Book Club subscribers to this series. Overseas and Eire please write for details and readers in Southern Africa write to Box 3010, Pinegowie, 2123 RSA. We reserve the right to refuse an application and applicants must be aged 18 years or over. Only one application per household. Terms and prices subject to change without notice. Offer expires 31st March 2009. As a result of this application, you may receive offers from Harlequin Mills & Boon and other carefully selected companies. If you would prefer not to share in this opportunity please write to The Data Manager, PO Box 676, Richmond, TW9 1WU.

Mills & Boon® is a registered trademark owned by Harlequin Mills & Boon Limited.
The Mills & Boon® Book Club™ is being used as a trademark.